CONTENTS

Modern Vintage Publishing edition, 2023.

SCARY CHRISTMAS

The Christmas Book of Short Scary Stories and Tiny Terrifying Tales

Edited by John Cooper

FOREWORD

Welcome to "Scary Christmas," an anthology of short stories that aims to defy the comforting glow of yuletide festivities with a chilling twist. This collection brings together the haunting echoes of classic tales woven with the fresh, spine-tingling narratives penned by emerging authors from around the globe.

Within these pages lie an array of shivers—a mix of classic ghost stories from the pens of literary luminaries of the past, festive terrors, and psychological thrills from innovative voices of modern storytellers—blending the warmth of the season with a bone-chilling ambiance, each tale crafted to leave an indelible mark on the holiday spirit.

Prepare to embark on a journey that will unsettle the most festive of spirits, making this holiday season one you won't soon forget. Welcome to a Christmas unlike any other—a season of jingles and frights, warmth and chills—a Scary Christmas.

THE SHADOWED SCHEME IN LAPLAND

By Macie Atkins

The story "How Nuth would have Practised his Art upon the Gnoles" emerged within the pages of 'The Book of Wonder', penned by Lord Dunsany in 1912. This was the seventh book and the fifth collection of original short stories by the prolific Irish fantasy writer and dramatist. Notably, Dunsany's imaginative genius has left a profound mark on the creations of influential authors like J.R.R. Tolkien, H.P. Lovecraft, Ursula K. Le Guin, and several others. The story and characteristics were likely the origin of the gnoll, used in a number of later works, notably within the Dungeons and Dragons and Warhammer universes.

Many decades later the writer Margaret St. Clair would use the tale as inspiration for "The Man who sold rope to the Gnoles" and here in a new century, in a new composition for this anthology, British author Macie Atkins has returned to the original text to re-work the story and set the protagonist upon a new target, the elves within Santa Claus workshop. Atkins assures me that Nuth, now named Mr. Cooper, has not been titled for your esteemed editor.

THE SHADOWED SCHEME IN LAPLAND

In the hushed corners of the market, whispers swirled around the prowess of Mr. Cooper. An enigmatic figure, his name shared amongst a chosen few, a shadow in the trade unseen by the common eye. Cooper didn't peddle his skills like the rest; he was the clandestine maestro of an intricate dance in the world of business, a burglar unmatched by any modern standard.

His prowess? Unrivalled. His terms? A calculated game of cash and covert transactions. His skill? A symphony in the night, quieter than the breeze through an empty street. Cooper lived in the shadows, a master craftsman in the art of thievery.

Picture it—those who ventured into stately manors, eyeing treasures they dared not claim. They'd whisper tales of Cooper's finesse, the quiet precision with which he sculpted theft into an art. Tapestries, relics, heirlooms—all fell under his quiet expertise. The touch of his hands would leave the room clean, the theft an artistry unnoticed.

It's a peculiar sight, these ostentatious mansions filled with the remnants of past lives. A side glance reveals the handiwork of the incomparable Cooper—a testament to the whispered whispers and the secrets held tight within the folds of the night.

Its not like I'm Cooper's buddy, not one bit. My game is property, always has been. But Cooper? He ain't needing my words, 'cause he's in a league of his own, in a world where advertising ain't his game.

This story kicks off in Belgrave Square, Cooper's turf, a place he's spun his magic, in a grand old house, on the market for years. He's got a knack for making friends, even with the caretaker. That joint fits him like a glove, and when folks come round to check it out, that caretaker's got lines straight out of Cooper's play-book. "Finest house in London," she'd sing, throwing in a “but for the drains” and when they pounced on this remark and asked questions about the drains, she’d answer them that the drains also were good, but not so good as the house. Those visitors didn't lay eyes on Cooper, but you bet your bottom dollar, Cooper was there.

On a crisp winter morning, in a neat black dress, there shuffled in an old lady with a crimson-lined bonnet, seeking out Mr. Cooper. At her side, a giant of a son tagged along. Mrs. Bramblethorn, the caretaker, threw a glance up the street before ushering them in, leaving them to linger among the shrouded furniture in the drawing-room. Time ticked by, and then the room carried the aroma of a sweet scented vape, an unmistakable sign of Cooper's presence.

"Good Lord!," gasped the old lady, her bonnet's crimson brim twitching, "you about made me leap out of my skin." And in those eyes of his, she knew she'd misspoke in front of Mr. Cooper.

Finally, Cooper spoke up, and the old lady stammered out, all nerves and jitters, that her lad was a promising sort, had dabbled in the business, but craved more, and she reckoned Mr. Cooper could teach him a thing or two for a livelihood.

First-off, Cooper demanded a business reference. When presented one from a jeweller, with whom he was tight as a glove in their dealings, the end result was Cooper agreeing to take on young Rascalby (for that was the lad’s surname) and mould him into an apprentice. The old woman with the crimson-lined bonnet returned to her humble cottage in the country, whispering to her old man each evening, “Rascalby, we best lock up tight come nightfall; Finnegan's gone and turned burglar."

The specifics of the lad's apprenticeship, I shan't trouble you with. Those in the trade know them well, others care not, and those with leisure, they'd fail to grasp the slow steps Finnegan Rascalby took. First, he learned to tread over bare boards, obstacles underfoot, mastering silence in the dark. Then came the ascent up creaky stairs, the art of opening doors without a creak, and finally, the skill of scaling heights unnoticed.

The business bloomed, whispers of Finnegan Rascalby's progress filling the pages sent laboriously by Cooper's hand to the old woman in her crimson-lined bonnet. Cooper ditched his writing lessons early, deeming forgery not his game, dismissing writing as mere waste. Then came the dealings with Lord Underwood at his Surrey residence. A Saturday night was chosen; it being the Sabbath for Lord Underwood's kin, and by eleven, the manor slumbered.

Five minutes shy of midnight, Finnigan Rascalby, schooled by Mr. Cooper's expertise, emerged bearing a pocketful of rings and jewelled cuff-links. It was light, but the jewellers of London couldn't match it without a special jaunt to Africa, leaving Lord Underwood scrambling to dress properly, his cuffs flapping as he moved.

The shadows clung tight to Cooper's name, not even a whisper daring to breathe it out. To claim it bruised his ego would sting some, for they'd argue his shrewd mind was immune to such pettiness. Let's just say it stoked the embers of his ingenuity, birthing a scheme no other burglar dared dream. It was a plan to raid the elves' workshop, laid out to Rascalby over a cuppa.

Had Rascalby not been dizzy with pride from their last heist, had he not idolized Cooper, maybe things would have been different. But hey, what's done is done. He tried to reason, to dodge the job, claimed it wasn't square. Yet, one chilly Winters morn, a storm brewing in the skies, they crept closer to the fabled workshop of

Santa Claus' elves.

Cooper, gauging emeralds against mundane stones, calculated the likely heft of the Christmas baubles nestled in the elven abode up in Lapland. Two giant emeralds were the goal, draped between them on a cloak. Yet, should the weight exceed, one had to hit the ground, and quick. Greed was Cooper's cautionary tale to Rascalby, warning that the jewels meant zilch until they were beyond the elves grasp.

Silent steps led the way, their mission set.

No trace marked the path toward the shadows of Lapland's woods; neither man nor beast had dared poach the elves' domain for a century. One didn't stray twice into the elves' glades. And in spite the jolly deeds carried out in the workshop within, the trees themselves were a foreboding sign, unlike the serene ones we plant ourselves.

The nearest village lay miles away, its houses turned away from the woods, not a single window facing in that direction. They didn't breathe a word of it there, a story untold elsewhere.

Into the thick of Lapland's woods trod Cooper and Finnigan Rascalby. No guns in hand. Rascalby had pleaded for a pistol, yet Cooper dismissed it with a warning that "a shot would bring the world crashing down on us." Nothing more needed to be said.

They traversed the woods, delving deeper as the day wore on. A poacher's skeleton hung nailed to an oak door; fairies darted away at their approach; once Rascalby snapped a dry stick underfoot, forcing them both to freeze for twenty long minutes. The sunset painted foreboding omens through the trees, and with the arrival of night, they stumbled towards the lean, lofty house where the secretive elves resided.

In that desolate abode of the elves, an eerie silence enveloped the unassuming structure. Rascalby's fading courage flickered with a hint of hope, but to Cooper's weathered senses, it was an ominous quietude, too otherworldly. The sky held a looming dread, worse than a spoken curse, affording Cooper the luxury of fearing the worst while hesitating in doubt. But even amidst his apprehension, he didn't abandon the plan.

He dispatched Rascalby, his apprentice, armed with the tools of their trade, up a ladder towards the old loft window. The moment Rascalby's fingers grazed the weathered boards, the ominous yet earthly silence twisted into an otherworldly hush akin to a ghoul's touch. Every breath Rascalby took seemed to violate that unnerving silence. His heart pounded like war drums, the aglet on his shoelace tapped on a ladder's rung, and the forest leaves held their breath. Rascalby wished for any sound, even from a mouse or a mole, but the woodland remained still, even Cooper was motionless.

Realization struck Rascalby in that moment; leaving the colossal emeralds and the elves' forbidding house was the only sane choice. He decided to flee this malevolent wood, retire from the thieving trade, and secure a serene life in the countryside. He descended quietly, signalling to Cooper. But the elves had watched him through devious holes bored in tree trunks. The otherworldly silence gave way to Rascalby's frantic screams as they snatched him from the ladder—shrieks that crescendoed into incoherence. Where they took him, one should not inquire; what they did with him, I shall not reveal.

With mild surprise etched on his face, Cooper observed from the edge of the house, rubbing his chin. The sly trick of the holes in the trees was a novelty to him. Then, deftly, he slipped away through the foreboding woods.

"And did they catch Cooper?" you inquire, gentle reader.

"Oh, no, my child" (for such a query is naive). "Nobody ever catches Cooper."

THE CANTERVILLE GHOST

By Oscar Wilde

Oscar Wilde's debut story, "The Canterville Ghost," presents a humorous tale of a ghost facing troubles from residents of the house he haunts, marking Wilde's initial publication in 'The Court and Society Review' (1887). The story revolves around an American family who have purchased a notably haunted English castle, tormenting the ghost—a deceased English nobleman—trapped within the house's walls after a tragic history involving murder. This amusing chronicle has seen multiple adaptations for both stage and screen.

THE CANTERVILLE GHOST

I

When Mr. Hiram B. Otis, the American Minister, bought Canterville Chase, every one told him he was doing a very foolish thing, as there was no doubt at all that the place was haunted. Indeed, Lord Canterville himself, who was a man of the most punctilious honour, had felt it his duty to mention the fact to Mr. Otis when they came to discuss terms.

'We have not cared to live in the place ourselves,' said Lord Canterville, 'since my grand-aunt, the Dowager Duchess of Bolton, was frightened into a fit, from which she never really recovered, by two skeleton hands being placed on her shoulders as she was dressing for dinner, and I feel bound to tell you, Mr. Otis, that the ghost has been seen by several living members of my family, as well as by the rector of the parish, the Rev. Augustus Dampier, who is a Fellow of King's College, Cambridge. After the unfortunate accident to the Duchess, none of our younger servants would stay with us, and Lady Canterville often got very little sleep at night, in consequence of the mysterious noises that came from the corridor and the library.'

'My Lord,' answered the Minister, 'I will take the furniture and the ghost at a valuation. I come from a modern country, where we have everything that money can buy; and with all our spry young fellows painting the Old World red, and carrying off your best actors and prima-donnas, I reckon that if there were such a thing as a ghost in Europe, we'd have it at home in a very short time in one of our public museums, or on the road as a show.'

'I fear that the ghost exists,' said Lord Canterville, smiling, 'though it may have resisted the overtures of your enterprising impresarios. It has been well known for three centuries, since 1584 in fact, and always makes its appearance before the death of any member of our family.'

'Well, so does the family doctor for that matter, Lord Canterville. But there is no such thing, sir, as a ghost, and I guess the laws of Nature are not going to be suspended for the British aristocracy.'

'You are certainly very natural in America,' answered Lord Canterville, who did not quite understand Mr. Otis' last observation, 'and if you don't mind a ghost in the house, it is all right. Only you must remember I warned you.'

A few weeks after this, the purchase was concluded, and at the close of the season the Minister and his family went down to Canterville Chase. Mrs. Otis, who, as Miss Lucretia R. Tappan, of West 53rd Street, had been a celebrated New York belle, was now a very handsome, middle-aged woman, with fine eyes, and a superb profile. Many American ladies on leaving their native land adopt an appearance of chronic ill-health, under the impression that it is a form of European refinement, but Mrs. Otis had never fallen into this error. She had a magnificent constitution, and a really wonderful amount of animal spirits. Indeed, in many respects, she was quite English, and was an excellent example of the fact that we have really everything in common with America nowadays, except, of course, language.

Their eldest son, christened Washington by his parents in a moment of patriotism, which he never ceased to regret, was a fair-haired, rather good-looking young man, who had qualified himself for American diplomacy by leading the German at the Newport Casino for three successive seasons, and even in London was well known as an excellent dancer. Gardenias and the peerage were his only weaknesses. Otherwise he was extremely sensible.

Miss Virginia E. Otis was a little girl of fifteen, lithe and lovely as a fawn, and with a fine freedom in her large blue eyes. She was a wonderful amazon, and had once raced old Lord Bilton on her pony twice round the park, winning by a length and a half, just in front of the Achilles statue, to the huge delight of the young Duke of Cheshire, who proposed for her on the spot, and was sent back to Eton that very night by his guardians, in floods of tears.

After Virginia came the twins, who were usually called 'The Stars and Stripes,' as they were always getting swished. They were delightful boys, and with the exception of the worthy Minister the only true republicans of the family.

As Canterville Chase is seven miles from Ascot, the nearest railway station, Mr. Otis had telegraphed for a waggonette to meet them, and they started on their drive in high spirits. It was a lovely July evening, and the air was delicate with the scent of the pinewoods. Now and then they heard a wood pigeon brooding over its own sweet voice, or saw, deep in the rustling fern, the burnished breast of the pheasant. Little squirrels peered at them from the beech-trees as they went by, and the rabbits scudded away through the brushwood and over the mossy knolls, with their white tails in the air.

As they entered the avenue of Canterville Chase, however, the sky became suddenly overcast with clouds, a curious stillness seemed to hold the atmosphere, a great flight of rooks passed silently over their heads, and, before they reached the house, some big drops of rain had fallen.

Standing on the steps to receive them was an old woman, neatly dressed in black silk, with a white cap and apron. This was Mrs. Umney, the housekeeper, whom Mrs. Otis, at Lady Canterville's earnest request, had consented to keep on in her former position. She made them each a low curtsey as they alighted, and said in a quaint, old-fashioned manner, 'I bid you welcome to Canterville Chase.' Following her, they passed through the fine Tudor hall into the library, a long, low room, panelled in black oak, at the end of which was a large stained-glass window. Here they found tea laid out for them, and, after taking off their wraps, they sat down and began to look round, while Mrs. Umney waited on them.

Suddenly Mrs. Otis caught sight of a dull red stain on the floor just by the fireplace and, quite unconscious of what it really signified, said to Mrs. Umney, I am afraid something has been spilt there.

'Yes, madam,' replied the old housekeeper in a low voice, 'blood has been spilt on that spot.'

'How horrid,' cried Mrs. Otis; 'I don't at all care for bloodstains in a sitting-room. It must be removed at once.'

The old woman smiled, and answered in the same low, mysterious voice, 'It is the blood of Lady Eleanore de Canterville, who was murdered on that very spot by her own husband, Sir Simon de Canterville, in 1575. Sir Simon survived her nine years, and disappeared suddenly under very mysterious circumstances. His body has never been discovered, but his guilty spirit still haunts the Chase. The blood-stain has been much admired by tourists and others, and cannot be removed.'

'That is all nonsense,' cried Washington Otis; 'Pinkerton's Champion Stain Remover and Paragon Detergent will clean it up in no time,' and before the terrified housekeeper could interfere he had fallen upon his knees, and was rapidly scouring the floor with a small stick of what looked like a black cosmetic. In a few moments no trace of the blood-stain could be seen.

'I knew Pinkerton would do it,' he exclaimed triumphantly, as he looked round at his admiring family; but no sooner had he said these words than a terrible flash of lightning lit up the sombre room, a fearful peal of thunder made them all start to their feet, and Mrs. Umney fainted.

'What a monstrous climate!' said the American Minister calmly, as he lit a long cheroot. 'I guess the old country is so over-populated that they have not enough decent weather for everybody. I have always been of opinion that emigration is the only thing for England.

'My dear Hiram,' cried Mrs. Otis, 'what can we do with a woman who faints?'

'Charge it to her like breakages,' answered the Minister; 'she won't faint after that;' and in a few moments Mrs. Umney certainly came to. There was no doubt, however, that she was extremely upset, and she sternly warned Mr. Otis to beware of some trouble coming to the house.

'I have seen things with my own eyes, sir,' she said,'that would make any Christian's hair stand on end, and many and many a night I have not closed my eyes in sleep for the awful things that are done here.' Mr. Otis, however, and his wife warmly assured the honest soul that they were not afraid of ghosts, and, after invoking the blessings of Providence on her new master and mistress, and making arrangements for an increase of salary, the old housekeeper tottered off to her own room.

II

The storm raged fiercely all that night, but nothing of particular note occurred. The next morning, however, when they came down to breakfast, they found the terrible stain of blood once again on the floor. 'I don't think it can be the fault of the Paragon Detergent,' said Washington, 'for I have tried it with everything. It must be the ghost.' He accordingly rubbed out the stain a second time, but the second morning it appeared again. The third morning also it was there, though the library had been locked up at night by Mr. Otis himself, and the key carried upstairs.

The whole family were now quite interested; Mr. Otis began to suspect that he had been too dogmatic in his denial of the existence of ghosts, Mrs. Otis expressed her intention of joining the Psychical Society, and Washington prepared a long letter to Messrs. Myers and Podmore on the subject of the Permanence of Sanguineous Stains when connected with Crime.

That night all doubts about the objective existence of phantasmata were removed for ever.

The day had been warm and sunny; and, in the cool of the evening, the whole family went out to drive. They did not return home till nine o'clock, when they had a light supper.

The conversation in no way turned upon ghosts, so there were not even those primary conditions of receptive expectation which so often precede the presentation of psychical phenomena.

The subjects discussed, as I have since learned from Mr. Otis, were merely such as form the ordinary conversation of cultured

Americans of the better class, such as the immense superiority of Miss Fanny Davenport over Sara Bernhardt as an actress; the difficulty of obtaining green corn, buckwheat cakes, and hominy, even in the best English houses; the importance of Boston in the development of the world-soul; the advantages of the baggage check system in railway travelling; and the sweetness of the New York accent as compared to the London drawl.

No mention at all was made of the supernatural, nor was Sir Simon de Canterville alluded to in any way. At eleven o'clock the family retired, and by half-past all the lights were out. Some time after, Mr. Otis was awakened by a curious noise in the corridor, outside his room. It sounded like the clank of metal, and seemed to be coming nearer every moment.

He got up at once, struck a match, and looked at the time. It was exactly one o'clock. He was quite calm, and felt his pulse, which was not at all feverish. The strange noise still continued, and with it he heard distinctly the sound of footsteps. He put on his slippers, took a small oblong phial out of his dressing-case, and opened the door.

Right in front of him he saw, in the wan moonlight, an old man of terrible aspect. His eyes were as red burning coals; long grey hair fell over his shoulders in matted coils; his garments, which were of antique cut, were soiled and ragged, and from his wrists and ankles hung heavy manacles and rusty gyves.

'My dear sir,' said Mr. Otis,'I really must insist on your oiling those chains, and have brought you for that purpose a small bottle of the Tammany Rising Sun Lubricator. It is said to be completely efficacious upon one application, and there are several testimonials to that effect on the wrapper from some of our most eminent native divines. I shall leave it here for you by the bedroom candles, and will be happy to supply you with more should you require it.' With these words the United States

Minister laid the bottle down on a marble table, and, closing his door, retired to rest.

For a moment the Canterville ghost stood quite motionless in natural indignation; then, dashing the bottle violently upon the polished floor, he fled down the corridor, uttering hollow groans, and emitting a ghastly green light.

Just, however, as he reached the top of the great oak staircase, a door was flung open, two little white-robed figures appeared, and a large pillow whizzed past his head! There was evidently no time to be lost, so, hastily adopting the Fourth Dimension of Space as a means of escape, he vanished through the wainscoting, and the house became quite quiet.

On reaching a small secret chamber in the left wing, he leaned up against a moonbeam to recover his breath, and began to try and realise his position.

Never, in a brilliant and uninterrupted career of three hundred years, had he been so grossly insulted.

He thought of the Dowager Duchess, whom he had frightened into a fit as she stood before the glass in her lace and diamonds; of the four housemaids, who had gone off into hysterics when he merely grinned at them through the curtains of one of the spare bedrooms; of the rector of the parish, whose candle he had blown out as he was coming late one night from the library, and who had been under the care of Sir William Gull ever since, a perfect martyr to nervous disorders; and of old Madame de Tremouillac, who, having wakened up one morning early and seen a skeleton seated in an armchair by the fire reading her diary, had been confined to her bed for six weeks with an attack of brain fever, and, on her recovery, had become reconciled to the Church, and broken off her connection with that notorious sceptic Monsieur de Voltaire.

He remembered the terrible night when the wicked Lord

Canterville was found choking in his dressing-room, with the knave of diamonds half-way down his throat, and confessed, just before he died, that he had cheated Charles James Fox out of 50,000 at Crockford's by means of that very card, and swore that the ghost had made him swallow it.

All his great achievements came back to him again, from the butler who had shot himself in the pantry because he had seen a green hand tapping at the window pane, to the beautiful Lady Stutfield, who was always obliged to wear a black velvet band round her throat to hide the mark of five fingers burnt upon her white skin, and who drowned herself at last in the carp-pond at the end of the King's Walk.

With the enthusiastic egotism of the true artist he went over his most celebrated performances, and smiled bitterly to himself as he recalled to mind his last appearance as 'Red Reuben, or the Strangled Babe,' his debut as 'Gaunt Gibeon, the Blood-sucker of Bexley Moor,' and the furore he had excited one lovely June evening by merely playing ninepins with his own bones upon the lawn-tennis ground. And after all this, some wretched modern Americans were to come and offer him the Rising Sun Lubricator, and throw pillows at his head! It was quite unbearable. Besides, no ghost in history had ever been treated in this manner. Accordingly, he determined to have vengeance, and remained till daylight in an attitude of deep thought.

III

The next morning, when the Otis family met at breakfast, they discussed the ghost at some length. The United States Minister was naturally a little annoyed to find that his present had not been accepted. 'I have no wish,' he said, 'to do the ghost any personal injury, and I must say that, considering the length of time he has been in the house, I don't think it is at all polite to throw pillows at him' - a very just remark, at which, I am sorry to say, the twins burst into shouts of laughter. 'Upon the other hand,' he continued, 'if he really declines to use the Rising Sun Lubricator, we shall have to take his chains from him. It would be quite impossible to sleep, with such a noise going on outside the bedrooms.'

For the rest of the week, however, they were undisturbed, the only thing that excited any attention being the continual renewal of the blood-stain on the library floor. This certainly was very strange, as the door was always locked at night by Mr. Otis, and the windows kept closely barred.

The chameleon-like colour, also, of the stain excited a good deal of comment. Some mornings it was a dull (almost Indian) red, then it would be vermilion, then a rich purple, and once when they came down for family prayers, according to the simple rites of the Free American Reformed Episcopalian Church, they found it a bright emerald green. These kaleidoscopic changes naturally amused the party very much, and bets on the subject were freely made every evening. The only person who did not enter into the joke was little Virginia, who, for some unexplained reason, was always a good deal distressed at the sight of the blood-stain, and very nearly cried the morning it was emerald-green.

The second appearance of the ghost was on Sunday night.

Shortly after they had gone to bed they were suddenly alarmed by a fearful crash in the hall. Rushing downstairs, they found that a large suit of old armour had become detached from its stand, and had fallen on the stone floor, while, seated in a highbacked chair, was the Canterville ghost, rubbing his knees with an expression of acute agony on his face.

The twins, having brought their pea-shooters with them, at once discharged two pellets on him, with that accuracy of aim which can only be attained by long and careful practice on a writing-master, while the United States Minister covered him with his revolver, and called upon him, in accordance with Californian etiquette, to hold up his hands!

The ghost started up with a wild shriek of rage, and swept through them like a mist, extinguishing Washington Otis's candle as he passed, and so leaving them all in total darkness. On reaching the top of the staircase he recovered himself, and determined to give his celebrated peal of demoniac laughter. This he had on more than one occasion found extremely useful. It was said to have turned Lord Raker's wig grey in a single night, and had certainly made three of Lady Canterville's French governesses give warning before their month was up.

He accordingly laughed his most horrible laugh, till the old vaulted roof rang and rang again, but hardly had the fearful echo died away when a door opened, and Mrs. Otis came out in a light blue dressing-gown. 'I am afraid you are far from well,' she said, 'and have brought you a bottle of Dr. Dobell's tincture. If it is indigestion, you will find it a most excellent remedy.'

The ghost glared at her in fury, and began at once to make preparations for turning himself into a large black dog, an accomplishment for which he was justly renowned, and to which the family doctor always attributed the permanent idiocy of Lord Canterville's uncle, the Hon. Thomas Horton. The sound of approaching footsteps, however, made him hesitate in his fell purpose, so he contented himself with becoming faintly phosphorescent, and vanished with a deep churchyard groan, just as the twins had come up to him.

On reaching his room he entirely broke down, and became a prey to the most violent agitation. The vulgarity of the twins, and the gross materialism of Mrs. Otis, were naturally extremely annoying, but what really distressed him most was, that he had been unable to wear the suit of mail.

He had hoped that even modern Americans would be thrilled by the sight of a Spectre In Armour, if for no more sensible reason, at least out of respect for their national poet Longfellow, over whose graceful and attractive poetry he himself had whiled away many a weary hour when the Cantervilles were up in town. Besides, it was his own suit. He had worn it with great success at the Kenilworth tournament, and had been highly complimented on it by no less a person than the Virgin Queen herself.

Yet when he had put it on, he had been completely overpowered by the weight of the huge breastplate and steel casque, and had fallen heavily on the stone pavement, barking both his knees severely, and bruising the knuckles of his right hand.

For some days after this he was extremely ill, and hardly stirred out of his room at all, except to keep the blood-stain in proper repair. However, by taking great care of himself, he recovered, and resolved to make a third attempt to frighten the United States Minister and his family.

He selected Friday, the 17th of August, for his appearance, and spent most of that day in looking over his wardrobe, ultimately deciding in favour of a large slouched hat with a red feather, a winding-sheet frilled at the wrists and neck, and a rusty dagger.

Towards evening a violent storm of rain came on, and the wind was so high that all the windows and doors in the old house shook and rattled. In fact, it was just such weather as he loved.

His plan of action was this. He was to make his way quietly to Washington Otis's room, gibber at him from the foot of the bed, and stab himself three times in the throat to the sound of slow music. He bore Washington a special grudge, being quite aware that it was he who was in the habit of removing the famous Canterville blood-stain, by means of Pinkerton's Paragon Detergent.

Having reduced the reckless and foolhardy youth to a condition of abject terror, he was then to proceed to the room occupied by the United States Minister and his wife, and there to place a clammy hand on Mrs. Otis's forehead, while he hissed into her trembling husband's ear the awful secrets of the charnel-house.

With regard to little Virginia, he had not quite made up his mind. She had never insulted him in any way, and was pretty and gentle. A few hollow groans from the wardrobe, he thought, would be more than sufficient, or, if that failed to wake her, he might grabble at the counterpane with palsy-twitching fingers.

As for the twins, he was quite determined to teach them a lesson. The first thing to be done was, of course, to sit upon their chests, so as to produce the stifling sensation of nightmare. Then, as their beds were quite close to each other, to stand between them in the form of a green, icy-cold corpse, till they became paralysed with fear, and finally, to throw off the winding-sheet, and crawl round the room, with white, bleached bones and one rolling eyeball, in the character of 'Dumb Daniel, or the Suicide's Skeleton,' a role in which he had on more than one occasion produced a great effect, and which he considered quite equal to his famous part of 'Martin the Maniac, or the Masked Mystery.'

At half-past ten he heard the family going to bed. For some time he was disturbed by wild shrieks of laughter from the twins, who, with the light-hearted gaiety of schoolboys, were evidently amusing themselves before they retired to rest, but at a quarter past eleven all was still, and, as midnight sounded, he sallied forth.

The owl beat against the window panes, the raven croaked from the old yew-tree, and the wind wandered moaning round the house like a lost soul; but the Otis family slept unconscious of their doom, and high above the rain and storm he could hear the steady snoring of the Minister for the United States.

He stepped stealthily out of the wainscoting, with an evil smile on his cruel, wrinkled mouth, and the moon hid her face in a cloud as he stole past the great oriel window, where his own arms and those of his murdered wife were blazoned in azure and gold. On and on he glided, like an evil shadow, the very darkness seeming to loathe him as he passed. Once he thought he heard something call, and stopped; but it was only the baying of a dog from the Red Farm, and he went on, muttering strange sixteenth-century curses, and ever and anon brandishing the rusty dagger in the midnight air.

Finally he reached the corner of the passage that led to luckless Washington's room. For a moment he paused there, the wind blowing his long grey locks about his head, and twisting into grotesque and fantastic folds the nameless horror of the dead man's shroud. Then the clock struck the quarter, and he felt the time was come.

He chuckled to himself, and turned the corner; but no sooner had he done so, than, with a piteous wail of terror, he fell back, and hid his blanched face in his long, bony hands.

Right in front of him was standing a horrible spectre, motionless as a carven image, and monstrous as a madman's dream! Its head was bald and burnished; its face round, and fat, and white; and hideous laughter seemed to have writhed its features into an eternal grin. From the eyes streamed rays of scarlet light, the mouth was a wide well of fire, and a hideous garment, like to his own, swathed with its silent snows the Titan form. On its breast was a placard with strange writing in antique characters, some scroll of shame it seemed, some record of wild sins, some awful calendar of crime, and, with its right hand, it bore aloft a falchion of gleaming steel.

Never having seen a ghost before, he naturally was terribly frightened, and, after a second hasty glance at the awful phantom, he fled back to his room, tripping up in his long winding sheet as he sped down the corridor, and finally dropping the rusty dagger into the Minister's jack-boots, where it was found in the morning by the butler.

Once in the privacy of his own apartment, he flung himself down on a small pallet-bed, and hid his face under the clothes. After a time, however, the brave old Canterville spirit asserted itself, and he determined to go and speak to the other ghost as soon as it was daylight.

Accordingly, just as the dawn was touching the hills with silver, he returned towards the spot where he had first laid eyes on the grisly phantom, feeling that, after all, two ghosts were better than one, and that, by the aid of his new friend, he might safely grapple with the twins.

On reaching the spot, however, a terrible sight met his gaze. Something had evidently happened to the spectre, for the light had entirely faded from its hollow eyes, the gleaming falchion had fallen from its hand, and it was leaning up against the wall in a strained and uncomfortable attitude.

He rushed forward and seized it in his arms, when, to his horror, the head slipped off and rolled on the floor, the body assumed a recumbent posture, and he found himself clasping a white dimity bed-curtain, with a sweeping-brush, a kitchen cleaver, and a hollow turnip lying at his feet! Unable to understand this curious transformation, he clutched the placard with feverish haste, and there, in the grey morning light, he read these fearful words: -

YE OTIS GHOSTE.

Ye Onlie true and Originale Spook.

Beware of Ye Imitationes.

All others are Counterfeite.

The whole thing flashed across him. He had been tricked, foiled, and outwitted!

The old Canterville look came into his eyes; he ground his toothless gums together; and, raising his withered hands high above his head, swore, according to the picturesque phraseology of the antique school, that when Chanticleer had sounded twice his merry horn, deeds of blood would be wrought, and Murder walk abroad with silent feet.

Hardly had he finished this awful oath when, from the red-tiled roof of a distant homestead, a cock crew. He laughed a long, low, bitter laugh, and waited. Hour after hour he waited, but the cock, for some strange reason, did not crow again.

Finally, at half-past seven, the arrival of the housemaids made him give up his fearful vigil, and he stalked back to his room, thinking of his vain oath and baffled purpose. There he consulted several books of ancient chivalry, of which he was exceedingly fond, and found that, on every occasion on which his oath had been used, Chanticleer had always crowed a second time. 'Perdition seize the naughty fowl,' he muttered, 'I have seen the day when, with my stout spear, I would have run him through the gorge, and made him crow for me an 'twere in death!'

He then retired to a comfortable lead coffin, and stayed there till evening.

IV

The next day the ghost was very weak and tired. The terrible excitement of the last four weeks was beginning to have its effect. His nerves were completely shattered, and he started at the slightest noise.

For five days he kept his room, and at last made up his mind to give up the point of the blood-stain on the library floor. If the Otis family did not want it, they clearly did not deserve it. They were evidently people on a low, material plane of existence, and quite incapable of appreciating the symbolic value of sensuous phenomena.

The question of phantasmic apparitions, and the development of astral bodies, was of course quite a different matter, and really not under his control. It was his solemn duty to appear in the corridor once a week, and to gibber from the large oriel window on the first and third Wednesdays in every month, and he did not see how he could honourably escape from his obligations. It is quite true that his life had been very evil, but, upon the other hand, he was most conscientious in all things connected with the supernatural.

For the next three Saturdays, accordingly, he traversed the corridor as usual between midnight and three o'clock, taking every possible precaution against being either heard or seen. He removed his boots, trod as lightly as possible on the old worm-eaten boards, wore a large black velvet cloak, and was careful to use the Rising Sun Lubricator for oiling his chains.

I am bound to acknowledge that it was with a good deal of difficulty that he brought himself to adopt this last mode of protection. However, one night, while the family were at dinner, he slipped into Mr. Otis's bedroom and carried off the bottle. He felt a little humiliated at first, but afterwards was sensible enough to see that there was a great deal to be said for the invention, and, to a certain degree, it served his purpose.

Still, in spite of everything, he was not left unmolested. Strings were continually being stretched across the corridor, over which he tripped in the dark, and on one occasion, while dressed for the part of 'Black Isaac, or the Huntsman of Hogley Woods,' he met with a severe fall, through treading on a butter-slide, which the twins had constructed from the entrance of the Tapestry Chamber to the top of the oak staircase.

This last insult so enraged him, that he resolved to make one final effort to assert his dignity and social position, and determined to visit the insolent young Etonians the next night in his celebrated character of 'Reckless Rupert, or the Headless Earl.'

He had not appeared in this disguise for more than seventy years; in fact, not since he had so frightened pretty Lady Barbara Modish by means of it, that she suddenly broke off her engagement with the present Lord Canterville's grandfather, and ran away to Gretna Green with handsome Jack Castleton, declaring that nothing in the world would induce her to marry into a family that allowed such a horrible phantom to walk up and down the terrace at twilight.

Poor Jack was afterwards shot in a duel by Lord Canterville on Wandsworth Common, and Lady Barbara died of a broken heart at Tunbridge Wells before the year was out, so, in every way, it had been a great success.

It was, however, an extremely difficult 'make-up,' if I may use such a theatrical expression in connection with one of the greatest mysteries of the supernatural, or, to employ a more scientific term, the higher-natural world, and it took him fully three hours to make his preparations.

At last everything was ready, and he was very pleased with his appearance. The big leather riding-boots that went with the dress were just a little too large for him, and he could only find one of the two horse-pistols, but, on the whole, he was quite satisfied, and at a quarter past one he glided out of the wainscoting and crept down the corridor.

On reaching the room occupied by the twins, which I should mention was called the Blue Bed Chamber, on account of the colour of its hangings, he found the door just ajar. Wishing to make an effective entrance, he flung it wide open, when a heavy jug of water fell right down on him, wetting him to the skin, and just missing his left shoulder by a couple of inches. At the same moment he heard stifled shrieks of laughter proceeding from the four-post bed.

The shock to his nervous system was so great that he fled back to his room as hard as he could go, and the next day he was laid up with a severe cold. The only thing that at all consoled him in the whole affair was the fact that he had not brought his head with him, for, had he done so, the consequences might have been very serious.

He now gave up all hope of ever frightening this rude American family, and contented himself, as a rule, with creeping about the passages in his slippers, with a thick red muffler round his throat for fear of draughts, and a small arquebuse, in case he should be attacked by the twins.

The final blow he received occurred on the 19th of September. He had gone downstairs to the great entrance-hall, feeling sure that there, at any rate, he would be quite unmolested, and was amusing himself by making satirical remarks on the large Saroni photographs of the United States Minister and his wife, which had now taken the place of the Canterville family pictures.

He was simply but neatly clad in a long shroud, spotted with churchyard mould, had tied up his jaw with a strip of yellow linen, and carried a small lantern and a gravediggers's spade. In fact, he was dressed for the character of 'Jonas the Graveless, or the Corpse-Snatcher of Chertsey Barn,' one of his most remarkable impersonations, and one which the Cantervilles had every reason to remember, as it was the real origin of their quarrel with their neighbour, Lord Rufford.

It was about a quarter past two o'clock in the morning, and, as far as he could ascertain, no one was stirring. As he was strolling towards the library, however, to see if there were any traces left of the bloodstain, suddenly there leaped out on him from a dark corner two figures, who waved their arms wildly above their heads, and shrieked out 'BOO!' in his ear.

Seized with a panic, which, under the circumstances, was only natural, he rushed for the staircase, but found Washington Otis waiting for him there with the big garden-syringe; and being thus hemmed in by his enemies on every side, and driven almost to bay, he vanished into the great iron stove, which, fortunately for him, was not lit, and had to make his way home through the flues and chimneys, arriving at his own room in a terrible state of dirt, disorder, and despair.

After this he was not seen again on any nocturnal expedition. The twins lay in wait for him on several occasions, and strewed the passages with nutshells every night to the great annoyance of their parents and the servants, but it was of no avail. It was quite evident that his feelings were so wounded that he would not appear.

Mr. Otis consequently resumed his great work on the history of the Democratic Party, on which he had been engaged for some years; Mrs. Otis organised a wonderful clam-bake, which amazed the whole county; the boys took to lacrosse, euchre, poker, and other American national games; and Virginia rode about the lanes on her pony, accompanied by the young Duke of Cheshire, who had come to spend the last week of his holidays at Canterville Chase.

It was generally assumed that the ghost had gone away, and, in fact, Mr. Otis wrote a letter to that effect to Lord Canterville, who, in reply, expressed his great pleasure at the news, and sent his best congratulations to the Minister's worthy wife.

The Otises, however, were deceived, for the ghost was still in the house, and though now almost an invalid, was by no means ready to let matters rest, particularly as he heard that among the guests was the young Duke of Cheshire, whose grand-uncle, Lord Francis Stilton, had once bet a hundred guineas with Colonel Carbury that he would play dice with the Canterville ghost, and was found the next morning lying on the floor of the card-room in such a helpless paralytic state, that though he lived on to a great age, he was never able to say anything again but 'Double Sixes.'

The story was well known at the time, though, of course, out of respect to the feelings of the two noble families, every attempt was made to hush it up; and a full account of all the circumstances connected with it will be found in the third volume of Lord Tattle's 'Recollections of the Prince Regent and his Friends'.

The ghost, then, was naturally very anxious to show that he had not lost his influence over the Stiltons, with whom, indeed, he was distantly connected, his own first cousin having been married en secondes noces, the Sieur de Bulkeley, from whom, as every one knows, the Dukes of Cheshire are lineally descended.

Accordingly, he made arrangements for appearing to Virginia's little lover in his celebrated impersonation of 'The Vampire Monk, or, the Bloodless Benedictine,' a performance so horrible that when old Lady Startup saw it, which she did on one fatal New Year's Eve, in the year 1764, she went off into the most piercing shrieks, which culminated in violent apoplexy, and died in three days, after disinheriting the Cantervilles, who were her nearest relations, and leaving all her money to her London apothecary.

At the last moment, however, his terror of the twins prevented his leaving his room, and the little Duke slept in peace under the great feathered canopy in the Royal Bedchamber, and dreamed of Virginia.

V

A few days after this, Virginia and her curly-haired cavalier went out riding on Brockley meadows, where she tore her habit so badly in getting through a hedge, that, on their return home, she made up her mind to go up by the back staircase so as not to be seen.

As she was running past the Tapestry Chamber, the door of which happened to be open, she fancied she saw some one inside, and thinking it was her mother's maid, who sometimes used to bring her work there, looked in to ask her to mend her habit.

To her immense surprise, however, it was the Canterville Ghost himself! He was sitting by the window, watching the ruined gold of the yellowing trees fly through the air, and the red leaves dancing madly down the long avenue.

His head was leaning on his hand, and his whole attitude was one of extreme depression. Indeed, so forlorn, and so much out of repair did he look, that little Virginia, whose first idea had been to run away and lock herself in her room, was filled with pity, and determined to try and comfort him.

So light was her footfall, and so deep his melancholy, that he was not aware of her presence till she spoke to him.

'I am so sorry for you,' she said, 'but my brothers are going back to Eton tomorrow, and then, if you behave yourself, no one will annoy you.'

'It is absurd asking me to behave myself,' he answered, looking round in astonishment at the pretty little girl who had ventured to address him, quite absurd. I must rattle my chains, and groan through keyholes, and walk about at night, if that is what you mean. It is my only reason for existing.'

'It is no reason at all for existing, and you know you have been very wicked. Mrs. Umney told us, the first day we arrived here, that you had killed your wife.'

'Well, I quite admit it,' said the Ghost petulantly, 'but it was a purely family matter, and concerned no one else.'

'It is very wrong to kill any one,' said Virginia, who at times had a sweet Puritan gravity, caught from some old New England ancestor.

'Oh, I hate the cheap severity of abstract ethics! My wife was very plain, never had my ruffs properly starched, and knew nothing about cookery. Why, there was a buck I had shot in Hogley Woods, a magnificent pricket, and do you know how she had it sent up to table? However, it is no matter now, for it is all over, and I don't think it was very nice of her brothers to starve me to death, though I did kill her.'

'Starve you to death? Oh, Mr. Ghost, I mean Sir Simon, are you hungry? I have a sandwich in my case. Would you like it?'

'No, thank you, I never eat anything now; but it is very kind of you, all the same, and you are much nicer than the rest of your horrid, rude, vulgar, dishonest family.'

'Stop!' cried Virginia, stamping her foot, 'it is you who are rude, and horrid, and vulgar, and as for dishonesty, you know you stole the paints out of my box to try and furbish up that ridiculous blood-stain in the library.

First you took all my reds, including the vermilion, and I couldn't do any more sunsets, then you took the emerald-green and the chrome-yellow, and finally I had nothing left but indigo and Chinese white, and could only do moonlight scenes, which are always depressing to look at, and not at all easy to paint. I never told on you, though I was very much annoyed, and it was most ridiculous, the whole thing; for who ever heard of emerald-green blood?'

'Well, really,' said the Ghost, rather meekly, 'what was I to do? It is a very difficult thing to get real blood nowadays, and, as your brother began it all with his Paragon Detergent, I certainly saw no reason why I should not have your paints.

As for colour, that is always a matter of taste: the Cantervilles have blue blood, for instance, the very bluest in England; but I know you Americans don't care for things of this kind.'

'You know nothing about it, and the best thing you can do is to emigrate and improve your mind. My father will be only too happy to give you a free passage, and though there is a heavy duty on spirits of every kind, there will be no difficulty about the Custom House, as the officers are all Democrats.

Once in New York, you are sure to be a great success. I know lots of people there who would give a hundred thousand dollars to have a grandfather, and much more than that to have a family ghost.'

'I don't think I should like America.'

'I suppose because we have no ruins and no curiosities,' said Virginia satirically.

'No ruins! no curiosities!' answered the Ghost, 'you have your navy and your manners.'

'Good evening; I will go and ask papa to get the twins an extra week's holiday.'

'Please don't go, Miss Virginia,' he cried; I am so lonely and so unhappy, and I really don't know what to do. I want to go to sleep and I cannot.'

'That's quite absurd! You have merely to go to bed and blow out the candle. It is very difficult sometimes to keep awake, especially at church, but there is no difficulty at all about sleeping. Why, even babies know how to do that, and they are not very clever.'

'I have not slept for three hundred years,' he said sadly, and Virginia's beautiful blue eyes opened in wonder; 'for three hundred years I have not slept, and I am so tired.'

Virginia grew quite grave, and her little lips trembled like rose-leaves. She came towards him, and kneeling down at his side, looked up into his old withered face.

'Poor, poor Ghost,' she murmured, 'have you no place where you can sleep?'

'Far away beyond the pine woods,' he answered, in a low dreamy voice, 'there is a little garden. There the grass grows long and deep, there are the great white stars of the hemlock flower, there the nightingale sings all night long. All night long he sings, and the cold, crystal moon looks down, and the yew-tree spreads out its giant arms over the sleepers.'

Virginia's eyes grew dim with tears, and she hid her face in her hands.

'You mean the Garden of Death,' she whispered.

'Yes, Death. Death must be so beautiful. To lie in the soft brown earth, with the grasses waving above one's head, and listen to silence. To have no yesterday, and no to-morrow. To forget time, to forgive life, to be at peace. You can help me. You can open for me the portals of Death's house, for Love is always with you, and Love is stronger than Death is.'

Virginia trembled, a cold shudder ran through her, and for a few moments there was silence. She felt as if she was in a terrible dream.

Then the Ghost spoke again, and his voice sounded like the sighing of the wind.

'Have you ever read the old prophecy on the library window?'

'Oh, often,' cried the little girl, looking up; 'I know it quite well. It is painted in curious black letters, and it is difficult to read. There are only six lines:

Whan a golden girl can win

Prayer from out the lips of sin,

When the barren almond bears,

And a little child give away its tears,

Then shall all the house be still

And peace come to Canterville.

But I don't know what they mean.'

'They mean,' he said sadly, 'that you must weep with me for my sins, because I have no tears, and pray with me for my soul, because I have no faith, and then, if you have always been sweet, and good, and gentle, the Angel of Death will have mercy on me.

You will see fearful shapes in darkness, and wicked voices will whisper in your ear, but they will not harm you, for against the purity of a little child the powers of Hell cannot prevail.'

Virginia made no answer, and the Ghost wrung his hands in wild despair as he looked down at her bowed golden head. Suddenly she stood up, very pale, and with a strange light in her eyes. 'I am not afraid,' she said firmly, 'and I will ask the Angel to have mercy on you.'

He rose from his seat with a faint cry of joy, and taking her hand bent over it with old-fashioned grace and kissed it. His fingers were as cold as ice, and his lips burned like fire, but Virginia did not falter, as he led her across the dusky room.

On the faded green tapestry were broidered little huntsmen. They blew their tasselled horns and with their tiny hands waved to her to go back. 'Go back! little Virginia,' they cried, 'go back!' but the Ghost clutched her hand more tightly, and she shut her eyes against them. Horrible animals with lizard tails, and goggle eyes, blinked at her from the carven chimney-piece, and murmured 'Beware! little Virginia, beware! we may never see you again,' but the Ghost glided on more swiftly, and Virginia did not listen.

When they reached the end of the room he stopped, and muttered some words she could not understand. She opened her eyes, and saw the wall slowly fading away like a mist, and a great black cavern in front of her. A bitter cold wind swept round them, and she felt something pulling at her dress.

'Quick, quick,' cried the Ghost, 'or it will be too late,' and, in a moment, the wainscoting had closed behind them, and the Tapestry Chamber was empty.

VI

About ten minutes later, the bell rang for tea, and, as Virginia did not come down, Mrs. Otis sent up one of the footmen to tell her.

After a little time he returned and said that he could not find Miss Virginia anywhere.

As she was in the habit of going out to the garden every evening to get flowers for the dinner-table, Mrs. Otis was not at all alarmed at first, but when six o'clock struck, and Virginia did not appear, she became really agitated, and sent the boys out to look for her, while she herself and Mr. Otis searched every room in the house. At half past six the boys came back and said that they could find no trace of their sister anywhere.

They were all now in the greatest state of excitement, and did not know what to do, when Mr. Otis suddenly remembered that, some few days before, he had given a band of gipsies permission to camp in the park. He accordingly at once set off for Blackfell Hollow, where he knew they were, accompanied by his eldest son and two of the farm-servants. The little Duke of Cheshire, who was perfectly frantic with anxiety, begged hard to be allowed to go too, but Mr. Otis would not allow him, as he was afraid there might be a scuffle.

On arriving at the spot, however, he found that the gipsies had gone, and it was evident that their departure had been rather sudden, as the fire was still burning, and some plates were lying on the grass.

Having sent off Washington and the two men to scour the district, he ran home, and despatched telegrams to all the police inspectors in the county, telling them to look out for a little girl who had been kidnapped by tramps or gipsies. He then ordered his horse to be brought round, and, after insisting on his wife and the three boys sitting down to dinner, rode off down the Ascot road with a groom.

He had hardly, however, gone a couple of miles, when he heard somebody galloping after him, and, looking round, saw the little Duke coming up on his pony, with his face very flushed and no hat. 'I'm awfully sorry, Mr. Otis,' gasped out the boy, 'but I can't eat any dinner as long as Virginia is lost. Please, don't be angry with me; if you had let us be engaged last year, there would never have been all this trouble. You won't send me back, will you? I can't go! I won't go!'

The Minister could not help smiling at the handsome young scapegrace, and was a good deal touched at his devotion to Virginia, so leaning down from his horse, he patted him kindly on the shoulders, and said, 'Well, Cecil, if you won't go back I suppose you must come with me, but I must get you a hat at Ascot.'

'Oh, bother my hat! I want Virginia!' cried the little Duke, laughing, and they galloped on to the railway station. There Mr. Otis inquired of the station-master if any one answering to the description of Virginia had been seen on the platform, but could get no news of her.

The station-master, however, wired up and down the line, and assured him that a strict watch would be kept for her, and, after having bought a hat for the little Duke from a linen-draper, who was just putting up his shutters, Mr. Otis rode off to Bexley, a village about four miles away, which he was told was a well-known haunt of the gipsies, as there was a large common next to it. Here they roused up the rural policeman, but could get no information from him, and, after riding all over the common, they turned their horses' heads homewards, and reached the

Chase about eleven o'clock, dead-tired and almost heartbroken.

They found Washington and the twins waiting for them at the gate-house with lanterns, as the avenue was very dark. Not the slightest trace of Virginia had been discovered. The gipsies had been caught on Brockley meadows, but she was not with them, and they had explained their sudden departure by saying that they had mistaken the date of Chorton Fair, and had gone off in a hurry for fear they might be late.

Indeed, they had been quite distressed at hearing of Virginia's disappearance, as they were very grateful to Mr. Otis for having allowed them to camp in his park, and four of their number had stayed behind to help in the search. The carp-pond had been dragged, and the whole Chase thoroughly gone over, but without any result.

It was evident that, for that night at any rate, Virginia was lost to them; and it was in a state of the deepest depression that Mr. Otis and the boys walked up to the house, the groom following behind with the two horses and the pony.

In the hall they found a group of frightened servants, and lying on a sofa in the library was poor Mrs. Otis, almost out of her mind with terror and anxiety, and having her forehead bathed with eau-de-cologne by the old housekeeper. Mr. Otis at once insisted on her having something to eat, and ordered up supper for the whole party.

It was a melancholy meal, as hardly any one spoke, and even the twins were awestruck and subdued, as they were very fond of their sister. When they had finished, Mr. Otis, in spite of the entreaties of the little Duke, ordered them all to bed, saying that nothing more could be done that night, and that he would telegraph in the morning to Scotland Yard for some detectives to be sent down immediately.

Just as they were passing out of the dining-room, midnight

began to boom from the clock tower, and when the last stroke sounded they heard a crash and a sudden shrill cry; a dreadful peal of thunder shook the house, a strain of unearthly music floated through the air, a panel at the top of the staircase flew back with a loud noise, and out on the landing, looking very pale and white, with a little casket in her hand, stepped Virginia.

In a moment they had all rushed up to her. Mrs. Otis clasped her passionately in her arms, the Duke smothered her with violent kisses, and the twins executed a wild war-dance round the group.

'Good heavens! child, where have you been?' said Mr. Otis, rather angrily, thinking that she had been playing some foolish trick on them.'Cecil and I have been riding all over the country looking for you, and your mother has been frightened to death. You must never play these practical joks any more.'

'Except on the Ghost! except on the Ghost!' shrieked the twins, as they capered about.

'My own darling, thank God you are found; you must never leave my side again,' murmured Mrs. Otis, as she kissed the trembling child, and smoothed the tangled gold of her hair.

'Papa,' said Virginia quietly, 'I have been with the Ghost. He is dead, and you must come and see him. He had been very wicked, but he was really sorry for all that he had done, and he gave me this box of beautiful jewels before he died.'

The whole family gazed at her in mute amazement, but she was quite grave and serious; and, turning round, she led them through the opening in the wainscoting down a narrow secret corridor, Washington following with a lighted candle, which he had caught up from the table.

Finally, they came to a great oak door, studded with rusty nails. When Virginia touched it, it swung back on its heavy hinges, and they found themselves in a little low room, with a vaulted ceiling, and one tiny grated window.

Embedded in the wall was a huge iron ring, and chained to it was a gaunt skeleton, that was stretched out at full length on the stone floor, and seemed to be trying to grasp with its long fleshless fingers an old-fashioned trencher and ewer, that were placed just out of its reach.

The jug had evidently been once filled with water, as it was covered inside with green mould. There was nothing on the trencher but a pile of dust. Virginia knelt down beside the skeleton, and, folding her little hands together, began to pray silently, while the rest of the party looked on in wonder at the terrible tragedy whose secret was now disclosed to them.'

'Hallo!' suddenly exclaimed one of the twins, who had been looking out of the window to try and discover in what wing of the house the room was situated.

'Hallo! the old withered almond tree has blossomed. I can see the flowers quite plainly in the moonlight.'

'God has forgiven him,' said Virginia gravely, as she rose to her feet, and a beautiful light seemed to illumine her face.

'What an angel you are!' cried the young Duke, and he put his arm round her neck, and kissed her.

VII

Four days after these curious incidents a funeral started from Canterville Chase at about eleven o'clock at night. The hearse was drawn by eight black horses, each of which carried on its head a great tuft of nodding ostrich-plumes, and the leaden coffin was covered by a rich purple pall, on which was embroidered in gold the Canterville coat-of-arms.

By the side of the hearse and the coaches walked the servants with lighted torches, and the whole procession was wonderfully impressive.

Lord Canterville was the chief mourner, having come up specially from Wales to attend the funeral, and sat in the first carriage along with little Virginia. Then came the United States Minister and his wife, then Washington and the three boys, and in the last carriage was Mrs. Umney. It was generally felt that, as she had been frightened by the ghost for more than fifty years of her life, she had a right to see the last of him.

A deep grave had been dug in the corner of the churchyard, just under the old yew-tree, and the service was read in the most impressive manner by the Rev. Augustus Dampier. When the ceremony was over, the servants, according to an old custom observed in the Canterville family, extinguished their torches, and, as the coffin was being lowered into the grave, Virginia stepped forward, and laid on it a large cross made of white and pink almond-blossoms. As she did so, the moon came out from behind a cloud, and flooded with its silent silver the little churchyard, and from a distant copse a nightingale began to sing.

She thought of the ghost's description of the Garden of Death, her eyes became dim with tears, and she hardly spoke a word during the drive home.

The next morning, before Lord Canterville went up to town, Mr. Otis had an interview with him on the subject of the jewels the ghost had given to Virginia. They were perfectly magnificent, especially a certain ruby necklace with old Venetian setting, which was really a superb specimen of sixteenth-century work, and their value was so great that Mr. Otis felt considerable scruples about allowing his daughter to accept them.

'My Lord,' he said, 'I know that in this country mortmain is held to apply to trinkets as well as to land, and it is quite clear to me that these jewels are, or should be, heirlooms in your family. I must beg you, accordingly, to take them to London with you, and to regard them simply as a portion of your property which has been restored to you under certain strange conditions.

As for my daughter, she is merely a child, and has as yet, I am glad to say, but little interest in such appurtenances of idle luxury. I am also informed by Mrs. Otis, who, I may say, is no mean authority upon Art - having had the privilege of spending several winters in Boston when she was a girl - that these gems are of great monetary worth, and if offered for sale would fetch a tall price.

Under these circumstances, Lord Canterville, I feel sure that you will recognise how impossible it would be for me to allow them to remain in the possession of any member of my family; and, indeed, all such vain gauds and toys, however suitable or necessary to the dignity of the British aristocracy, would be completely out of place among those who have been brought up on the severe, and I believe immortal, principles of Republican simplicity.

Perhaps I should mention that Virginia is very anxious that

you should allow her to retain the box, as a memento of your unfortunate but misguided ancestor. As it is extremely old, and consequently a good deal out of repair, you may perhaps think fit to comply with her request.

For my own part, I confess I am a good deal surprised to find a child of mine expressing sympathy with mediaevalism in any form, and can only account for it by the fact that Virginia was born in one of your London suburbs shortly after Mrs. Otis had returned from a trip to Athens.

Lord Canterville listened very gravely to the worthy Minister's speech, pulling his grey moustache now and then to hide an involuntary smile, and when Mr. Otis had ended, he shook him cordially by the hand, and said, 'My dear sir, your charming little daughter rendered my unlucky ancestor, Sir Simon, a very important service, and I and my family are much indebted to her for her marvellous courage and pluck. The jewels are clearly hers, and, egad, I believe that if I were heartless enough to take them from her, the wicked old fellow would be out of his grave in a fortnight, leading me the devil of a life.

As for their being heirlooms, nothing is an heirloom that is not so mentioned in a will or legal document, and the existence of these jewels has been quite unknown. I assure you I have no more claim on them than your butler, and when Miss Virginia grows up I daresay she will be pleased to have pretty things to wear.

Besides, you forget, Mr. Otis, that you took the furniture and the ghost at a valuation, and anything that belonged to the ghost passed at once into your possession, as, whatever activity Sir Simon may have shown in the corridor at night, in point of law he was really dead, and you acquired his property by purchase.'

Mr. Otis was a good deal distressed at Lord Canterville's refusal, and begged him to reconsider his decision, but the good-natured peer was quite firm, and finally induced the Minister to allow his daughter to retain the present the ghost had given her, and when, in the spring of 1890, the young Duchess of Cheshire was presented at the Queen's first drawing-room on the occasion of her marriage, her jewels were the universal theme of admiration. For Virginia received the coronet, which is the reward of all good little American girls, and was married to her boy-lover as soon as he came of age.

They were both so charming, and they loved each other so much, that every one was delighted at the match, except the old Marchioness of Dumbleton, who had tried to catch the Duke for one of her seven unmarried daughters, and had given no less than three expensive dinner-parties for that purpose, and, strange to say, Mr. Otis himself.

Mr. Otis was extremely fond of the young Duke personally, but, theoretically, he objected to titles, and, to use his own words, 'was not without apprehension lest, amid the enervating influences of a pleasure-loving aristocracy, the true principles of Republican simplicity should be forgotten.'

His objections, however, were completely overruled, and I believe that when he walked up the aisle of St. George's, Hanover Square, with his daughter leaning on his arm, there was not a prouder man in the whole length and breadth of England.

The Duke and Duchess, after the honeymoon was over, went down to Canterville Chase, and on the day after their arrival they walked over in the afternoon to the lonely churchyard by the pine-woods. There had been a great deal of difficulty at first about the inscription on Sir Simon's tombstone, but finally it had been decided to engrave on it simply the initials of the old gentleman's name, and the verse from the library window.

The Duchess had brought with her some lovely roses, which she strewed upon the grave, and after they had stood by it for some time they strolled into the ruined chancel of the old abbey. There the Duchess sat down on a fallen pillar, while her husband lay at her feet smoking a cigarette and looking up at her beautiful eyes. Suddenly he threw his cigarette away, took hold of her hand, and said to her,'Virginia, a wife should have no secrets from her husband.

'Dear Cecil! I have no secrets from you.'

'Yes, you have,' he answered, smiling, 'you have never told me what happened to you when you were locked up with the ghost.'

'I have never told any one, Cecil,' said Virginia gravely.

'I know that, but you might tell me.'

'Please don't ask me, Cecil, I cannot tell you. Poor Sir Simon! I owe him a great deal. Yes, don't laugh, Cecil, I really do. He made me see what Life is, and what Death signifies, and why Love is stronger than both.'

The Duke rose and kissed his wife lovingly.

'You can have your secret as long as I have your heart,' he murmured.

'You have always had that, Cecil.

'And you will tell our children some day, won't you?'

Virginia blushed.

SCENE 2

By Jasper M Smith

In our sister anthology 'Yuletide Tales', Welsh author Jasper M Smith took us into a cozy pub nestled amidst the wintry night to show a scene of a spirited conversation on the season's enchantment, here, appearing for the first time in this anthology, in "Scene 2" he paints a somewhat darker scene.

SCENE 2

INTERIOR THE RED LION PUB – NIGHT

The pub is dimly lit and eerily quiet, old-fashioned lanterns cast distorted shadows that dance on the walls, creating shapes that seem to shift and morph in the dim light. The fire crackles loudly, occasionally sending sparks flying into the air. The air, thick with the smell of roasted chestnuts, carries an undercurrent of something inexplicably chilling.

PERSON 1, a weary figure with a haunted look in his eyes, slumps over the bar. His coat seems tattered, almost as if it's bearing the weight of the world itself. PERSON 2, a stout man with a white beard and a peculiar gleam in his eye that hints at something otherworldly, sits beside him, a glass of sherry untouched in front of him.

PERSON 1
(husky voice)
Christmas. Bah, it's all a farce. This idea of jolly spirits and miracles. Nothing but a mirage in a desert of reality.

PERSON 2
(smiling knowingly)
But sometimes, my friend, the mirage is more real than the desert itself.

PERSON 1
(glares)
What do you know about it?

PERSON 2

(leaning closer)
I've seen things that would make your blood run cold. Things that defy the rational mind.

PERSON 1
(scornful)
Like what? Ghosts of Christmas past?

PERSON 2
(voice lowering)
Not just ghosts. There are beings that lurk in the shadows, unseen but ever-present. Spirits that weave through our world, especially on a night like this.

PERSON 1
(eyes widening)
You can't be serious.

PERSON 2
(solemn)
Serious as a winter storm, my friend. There's magic in the air tonight, more than you can fathom.

PERSON 1
(scoffs)
Magic? In this dingy pub?

PERSON 2
(suddenly serious)
Magic that dances between the flames, whispers in the wind, and takes shape in the most unexpected ways.

PERSON 1
(tense)
What are you talking about?

PERSON 2
(gazes into the fire)
Tonight, the veil between worlds thins. And those who seek can

find what they need.

PERSON 1
(baffled)
What do you mean?

Before PERSON 2 can answer, a chilling gust blows through the cracks in the pub's walls, causing the flames to flicker wildly. The door creaks open, revealing a blizzard raging outside. A figure, barely discernible through the whirling snow, stands ominously framed in the doorway.

PERSON 2
(rising slowly)
He's here.

PERSON 1
(alarmed)
Who's here?

PERSON 2
(barely audible)
The sleigh master. He's come for what's been lost.

As the figure retreats into the storm, the fire roars unnaturally high for a moment, casting elongated shadows that seem to reach for PERSON 1. When the flames settle, PERSON 2 is gone, leaving PERSON 1 alone, the door swinging in the howling wind.

FADE OUT.

AN ACCOUNT OF SOME STRANGE DISTURBANCES IN AUNGIER STREET

By Joseph Sheridan Le Fanu

Aungier Street, pronounced AIN-jur – rhymes with "danger". This short story, by Irish writer of Gothic tales JS Le Fanu and first published in 1853 is celebrated for its uniqueness among Victorian ghost stories, standing out for its departure from the more moralistic narratives of the time (see Dickens for instance).

The story skillfully teaches how to create a gripping ghost tale, aiming more for entertainment than literary depth. It begins with a humble note, suggesting the best way to enjoy it is through live storytelling; the second best of course to be from a book, curled up by the fireside...

AN ACCOUNT OF SOME STRANGE DISTURBANCES IN AUNGIER STREET

It is not worth telling, this story of mine—at least, not worth writing. Told, indeed, as I have sometimes been called upon to tell it, to a circle of intelligent and eager faces, lighted up by a good after-dinner fire on a winter's evening, with a cold wind rising and wailing outside, and all snug and cosy within, it has gone off—though I say it, who should not—indifferent well. But it is a venture to do as you would have me. Pen, ink, and paper are cold vehicles for the marvellous, and a "reader" decidedly a more critical animal than a "listener." If, however, you can induce your friends to read it after nightfall, and when the fireside talk has run for a while on thrilling tales of shapeless terror; in short, if you will secure me the time, I will go to my work, and say my say, with better heart. Well, then, these conditions presupposed, I shall waste no more words, but tell you simply how it all happened.

My cousin (Tom Ludlow) and I studied medicine together. I think he would have succeeded, had he stuck to the profession; but he preferred the Church, poor fellow, and died early, a sacrifice to contagion, contracted in the noble discharge of his duties. For my present purpose, I say enough of his character when I mention that he was of a sedate but frank and cheerful nature; very exact in his observance of truth, and not by any means like myself—of an excitable or nervous temperament.

My Uncle Ludlow—Tom's father—while we were attending lectures, purchased three or four old houses in Aungier Street, one of which was unoccupied. He resided in the country, and Tom proposed that we should take up our abode in the untenanted house, so long as it should continue unlet; a move which would accomplish the double end of settling us nearer alike to our lecture-rooms and to our amusements, and of relieving us from the weekly charge of rent for our lodgings.

Our furniture was very scant—our whole equipage remarkably modest and primitive; and, in short, our arrangements pretty nearly as simple as those of a bivouac. Our new plan was, therefore, executed almost as soon as conceived. The front drawing-room was our sitting-room. I had the bedroom over it, and Tom the back bedroom on the same floor, which nothing could have induced me to occupy.

The house, to begin with, was a very old one. It had been, I believe, newly fronted about fifty years before; but with this exception, it had nothing modern about it. The agent who bought it and looked into the titles for my uncle, told me that it was sold, along with much other forfeited property, at Chichester House, I think, in 1702; and had belonged to Sir Thomas Hacket, who was Lord Mayor of Dublin in James II.'s time. How old it was then, I can't say; but, at all events, it had seen years and changes enough to have contracted all that mysterious and saddened air, at once exciting and depressing, which belongs to most old mansions.

There had been very little done in the way of modernising details; and, perhaps, it was better so; for there was something queer and by-gone in the very walls and ceilings—in the shape of doors and windows—in the odd diagonal site of the chimney-pieces—in the beams and ponderous cornices—not to mention the singular solidity of all the woodwork, from the banisters to the window-frames, which hopelessly defied disguise, and would have emphatically proclaimed their antiquity through any conceivable amount of modern finery and varnish.

An effort had, indeed, been made, to the extent of papering the drawing-rooms; but somehow, the paper looked raw and out of keeping; and the old woman, who kept a little dirt-pie of a shop in the lane, and whose daughter—a girl of two and fifty—was our solitary handmaid, coming in at sunrise, and chastely receding again as soon as she had made all ready for tea in our state apartment;—this woman, I say, remembered it, when old Judge Horrocks (who, having earned the reputation of a particularly "hanging judge," ended by hanging himself, as the coroner's jury found, under an impulse of "temporary insanity," with a child's skipping-rope, over the massive old bannisters) resided there, entertaining good company, with fine venison and rare old port. In those halcyon days, the drawing-rooms were hung with gilded leather, and, I dare say, cut a good figure, for they were really spacious rooms.

The bedrooms were wainscoted, but the front one was not gloomy; and in it the cosiness of antiquity quite overcame its sombre associations. But the back bedroom, with its two queerly-placed melancholy windows, staring vacantly at the foot of the bed, and with the shadowy recess to be found in most old houses in Dublin, like a large ghostly closet, which, from congeniality of temperament, had amalgamated with the bedchamber, and dissolved the partition. At night-time, this "alcove"—as our "maid" was wont to call it—had, in my eyes, a specially sinister and suggestive character. Tom's distant and solitary candle glimmered vainly into its darkness. There it was always overlooking him—always itself impenetrable. But this was only part of the effect. The whole room was, I can't tell how, repulsive to me. There was, I suppose, in its proportions and features, a latent discord—a certain mysterious and indescribable relation, which jarred indistinctly upon some secret sense of the fitting and the safe, and raised indefinable suspicions and apprehensions of the imagination. On the whole, as I began by saying, nothing could have induced me to pass a night alone in it.

I had never pretended to conceal from poor Tom my

superstitious weakness; and he, on the other hand, most unaffectedly ridiculed my tremors. The sceptic was, however, destined to receive a lesson, as you shall hear.

We had not been very long in occupation of our respective dormitories, when I began to complain of uneasy nights and disturbed sleep. I was, I suppose, the more impatient under this annoyance, as I was usually a sound sleeper, and by no means prone to nightmares. It was now, however, my destiny, instead of enjoying my customary repose, every night to "sup full of horrors." After a preliminary course of disagreeable and frightful dreams, my troubles took a definite form, and the same vision, without an appreciable variation in a single detail, visited me at least (on an average) every second night in the week.

Now, this dream, nightmare, or infernal illusion—which you please—of which I was the miserable sport, was on this wise:----

I saw, or thought I saw, with the most abominable distinctness, although at the time in profound darkness, every article of furniture and accidental arrangement of the chamber in which I lay. This, as you know, is incidental to ordinary nightmare. Well, while in this clairvoyant condition, which seemed but the lighting up of the theatre in which was to be exhibited the monotonous tableau of horror, which made my nights insupportable, my attention invariably became, I know not why, fixed upon the windows opposite the foot of my bed; and, uniformly with the same effect, a sense of dreadful anticipation always took slow but sure possession of me. I became somehow conscious of a sort of horrid but undefined preparation going forward in some unknown quarter, and by some unknown agency, for my torment; and, after an interval, which always seemed to me of the same length, a picture suddenly flew up to the window, where it remained fixed, as if by an electrical attraction, and my discipline of horror then commenced, to last perhaps for hours. The picture thus mysteriously glued to the window-panes, was the portrait of an old man, in a crimson flowered silk dressing-gown, the folds of which I could now describe, with a countenance embodying a strange mixture of intellect, sensuality, and power, but withal sinister and full of malignant omen. His nose was hooked, like the beak of a vulture; his eyes large, grey, and prominent, and lighted up with a more than mortal cruelty and coldness. These features were surmounted by a crimson velvet cap, the hair that peeped from under which was white with age, while the eyebrows retained their original blackness. Well I remember every line, hue, and shadow of that stony countenance, and well I may! The gaze of this hellish visage was fixed upon me, and mine returned it with the inexplicable fascination of nightmare, for what appeared to me to be hours of agony. At last----

> The cock he crew, away then flew

the fiend who had enslaved me through the awful watches of the night; and, harassed and nervous, I rose to the duties of the day.

I had—I can't say exactly why, but it may have been from the exquisite anguish and profound impressions of unearthly horror, with which this strange phantasmagoria was associated—an insurmountable antipathy to describing the exact nature of my nightly troubles to my friend and comrade. Generally, however, I told him that I was haunted by abominable dreams; and, true to the imputed materialism of medicine, we put our heads together to dispel my horrors, not by exorcism, but by a tonic.

I will do this tonic justice, and frankly admit that the accursed portrait began to intermit its visits under its influence. What of that? Was this singular apparition—as full of character as of terror—therefore the creature of my fancy, or the invention of my poor stomach? Was it, in short, subjective (to borrow the technical slang of the day) and not the palpable aggression and intrusion of an external agent? That, good friend, as we will both admit, by no means follows. The evil spirit, who enthralled my senses in the shape of that portrait, may have been just as near me, just as energetic, just as malignant, though I saw him not. What means the whole moral code of revealed religion regarding the due keeping of our own bodies, soberness, temperance, etc.? here is an obvious connexion between the material and the invisible; the healthy tone of the system, and its unimpaired energy, may, for aught we can tell, guard us against influences which would otherwise render life itself terrific. The mesmerist and the electro-biologist will fail upon an average with nine patients out of ten—so may the evil spirit. Special conditions of the corporeal system are indispensable to the production of certain spiritual phenomena. The operation succeeds sometimes—sometimes fails—that is all.

I found afterwards that my would-be sceptical companion had his troubles too. But of these I knew nothing yet. One night, for a wonder, I was sleeping soundly, when I was roused by a step on the lobby outside my room, followed by the loud clang of what turned out to be a large brass candlestick, flung with all his force by poor Tom Ludlow over the banisters, and rattling with a rebound down the second flight of stairs; and almost concurrently with this, Tom burst open my door, and bounced into my room backwards, in a state of extraordinary agitation.

I had jumped out of bed and clutched him by the arm before I had any distinct idea of my own whereabouts. There we were—in our shirts—standing before the open door—staring through the great old banister opposite, at the lobby window, through which the sickly light of a clouded moon was gleaming.

"What's the matter, Tom? What's the matter with you? What the devil's the matter with you, Tom?" I demanded shaking him with nervous impatience.

He took a long breath before he answered me, and then it was not very coherently.

"It's nothing, nothing at all—did I speak?—what did I say?—where's the candle, Richard? It's dark; I—I had a candle!"

"Yes, dark enough," I said; "but what's the matter?—what is it?—why don't you speak, Tom?—have you lost your wits?—what is the matter?"

"The matter?—oh, it is all over. It must have been a dream—nothing at all but a dream—don't you think so? It could not be anything more than a dream."

"Of course" said I, feeling uncommonly nervous, "it was a dream."

"I thought," he said, "there was a man in my room, and—and I jumped out of bed; and—and—where's the candle?"

"In your room, most likely," I said, "shall I go and bring it?"

"No; stay here—don't go; it's no matter—don't, I tell you; it was all a dream. Bolt the door, Dick; I'll stay here with you—I feel nervous. So, Dick, like a good fellow, light your candle and open the window—I am in a shocking state."

I did as he asked me, and robing himself like Granuaile in one of my blankets, he seated himself close beside my bed.

Every body knows how contagious is fear of all sorts, but more especially that particular kind of fear under which poor Tom was at that moment labouring. I would not have heard, nor I believe would he have recapitulated, just at that moment, for half the world, the details of the hideous vision which had so unmanned him.

"Don't mind telling me anything about your nonsensical dream, Tom," said I, affecting contempt, really in a panic; "let us talk about something else; but it is quite plain that this dirty old house disagrees with us both, and hang me if I stay here any longer, to be pestered with indigestion and—and—bad nights, so we may as well look out for lodgings—don't you think so?—at once."

Tom agreed, and, after an interval, said----

"I have been thinking, Richard, that it is a long time since I saw my father, and I have made up my mind to go down to-morrow and return in a day or two, and you can take rooms for us in the meantime."

I fancied that this resolution, obviously the result of the vision which had so profoundly scared him, would probably vanish next morning with the damps and shadows of night. But I was mistaken. Off went Tom at peep of day to the country, having agreed that so soon as I had secured suitable lodgings, I was to recall him by letter from his visit to my Uncle Ludlow.

Now, anxious as I was to change my quarters, it so happened, owing to a series of petty procrastinations and accidents, that nearly a week elapsed before my bargain was made and my letter of recall on the wing to Tom; and, in the meantime, a trifling adventure or two had occurred to your humble servant, which, absurd as they now appear, diminished by distance, did certainly at the time serve to whet my appetite for change considerably.

A night or two after the departure of my comrade, I was sitting by my bedroom fire, the door locked, and the ingredients of a tumbler of hot whisky-punch upon the crazy spider-table; for, as the best mode of keeping the

Black spirits and white,

Blue spirits and grey,

with which I was environed, at bay, I had adopted the practice recommended by the wisdom of my ancestors, and "kept my spirits up by pouring spirits down." I had thrown aside my volume of Anatomy, and was treating myself by way of a tonic, preparatory to my punch and bed, to half-a-dozen pages of the Spectator, when I heard a step on the flight of stairs descending from the attics. It was two o'clock, and the streets were as silent as a churchyard—the sounds were, therefore, perfectly distinct. There was a slow, heavy tread, characterised by the emphasis and deliberation of age, descending by the narrow staircase from above; and, what made the sound more singular, it was plain that the feet which produced it were perfectly bare, measuring the descent with something between a pound and a flop, very ugly to hear.

I knew quite well that my attendant had gone away many hours before, and that nobody but myself had any business in the house. It was quite plain also that the person who was coming down stairs had no intention whatever of concealing his movements; but, on the contrary, appeared disposed to make even more noise, and proceed more deliberately, than was at all necessary. When the step reached the foot of the stairs outside my room, it seemed to stop; and I expected every moment to see my door open spontaneously, and give admission to the original of my detested portrait. I was, however, relieved in a few seconds by hearing the descent renewed, just in the same manner, upon the staircase leading down to the drawing-rooms, and thence, after another pause, down the next flight, and so on to the hall, whence I heard no more.

Now, by the time the sound had ceased, I was wound up, as they say, to a very unpleasant pitch of excitement. I listened, but there was not a stir. I screwed up my courage to a decisive experiment —opened my door, and in a stentorian voice bawled over the banisters, "Who's there?" There was no answer but the ringing of my own voice through the empty old house,—no renewal of the movement; nothing, in short, to give my unpleasant sensations a definite direction. There is, I think, something most disagreeably disenchanting in the sound of one's own voice under such circumstances, exerted in solitude, and in vain. It redoubled my sense of isolation, and my misgivings increased on perceiving that the door, which I certainly thought I had left open, was closed behind me; in a vague alarm, lest my retreat should be cut off, I got again into my room as quickly as I could, where I remained in a state of imaginary blockade, and very uncomfortable indeed, till morning.

Next night brought no return of my barefooted fellow-lodger; but the night following, being in my bed, and in the dark —somewhere, I suppose, about the same hour as before, I distinctly heard the old fellow again descending from the garrets.

This time I had had my punch, and the morale of the garrison was consequently excellent. I jumped out of bed, clutched the poker as I passed the expiring fire, and in a moment was upon the lobby. The sound had ceased by this time—the dark and chill were discouraging; and, guess my horror, when I saw, or thought I saw, a black monster, whether in the shape of a man or a bear I could not say, standing, with its back to the wall, on the lobby, facing me, with a pair of great greenish eyes shining dimly out. Now, I must be frank, and confess that the cupboard which displayed our plates and cups stood just there, though at the moment I did not recollect it. At the same time I must honestly say, that making every allowance for an excited imagination, I never could satisfy myself that I was made the dupe of my own fancy in this matter; for this apparition, after one or two shiftings of shape, as if in the act of incipient transformation, began, as it seemed on second thoughts, to advance upon me in its original form. From an instinct of terror rather than of courage, I hurled the poker, with all my force, at its head; and to the music of a horrid crash made my way into my room, and double-locked the door. Then, in a minute more, I heard the horrid bare feet walk down the stairs, till the sound ceased in the hall, as on the former occasion.

If the apparition of the night before was an ocular delusion of my fancy sporting with the dark outlines of our cupboard, and if its horrid eyes were nothing but a pair of inverted teacups, I had, at all events, the satisfaction of having launched the poker with admirable effect, and in true "fancy" phrase, "knocked its two daylights into one," as the commingled fragments of my tea-service testified. I did my best to gather comfort and courage from these evidences; but it would not do. And then what could I say of those horrid bare feet, and the regular tramp, tramp, tramp, which measured the distance of the entire staircase through the solitude of my haunted dwelling, and at an hour when no good influence was stirring? Confound it!--the whole affair was abominable. I was out of spirits, and dreaded the approach of night.

It came, ushered ominously in with a thunder-storm and dull torrents of depressing rain. Earlier than usual the streets grew silent; and by twelve o'clock nothing but the comfortless pattering of the rain was to be heard.

I made myself as snug as I could. I lighted two candles instead of one. I forswore bed, and held myself in readiness for a sally, candle in hand; for, coûte qui coûte, I was resolved to see the being, if visible at all, who troubled the nightly stillness of my mansion. I was fidgetty and nervous and tried in vain to interest myself with my books. I walked up and down my room, whistling in turn martial and hilarious music, and listening ever and anon for the dreaded noise. I sate down and stared at the square label on the solemn and reserved-looking black bottle, until "FLANAGAN & CO'S BEST OLD MALT WHISKY" grew into a sort of subdued accompaniment to all the fantastic and horrible speculations which chased one another through my brain.

Silence, meanwhile, grew more silent, and darkness darker. I listened in vain for the rumble of a vehicle, or the dull clamour of a distant row. There was nothing but the sound of a rising wind, which had succeeded the thunder-storm that had travelled over the Dublin mountains quite out of hearing. In the middle of this great city I began to feel myself alone with nature, and Heaven knows what beside. My courage was ebbing. Punch, however, which makes beasts of so many, made a man of me again—just in time to hear with tolerable nerve and firmness the lumpy, flabby, naked feet deliberately descending the stairs again.

I took a candle, not without a tremour. As I crossed the floor I tried to extemporise a prayer, but stopped short to listen, and never finished it. The steps continued. I confess I hesitated for some seconds at the door before I took heart of grace and opened it. When I peeped out the lobby was perfectly empty—there was no monster standing on the staircase; and as the detested sound ceased, I was reassured enough to venture forward nearly to the banisters. Horror of horrors! within a stair or two beneath the spot where I stood the unearthly tread smote the floor. My eye caught something in motion; it was about the size of Goliah's foot—it was grey, heavy, and flapped with a dead weight from one step to another. As I am alive, it was the most monstrous grey rat I ever beheld or imagined.

Shakespeare says—"Some men there are cannot abide a gaping pig, and some that are mad if they behold a cat." I went well-nigh out of my wits when I beheld this rat; for, laugh at me as you may, it fixed upon me, I thought, a perfectly human expression of malice; and, as it shuffled about and looked up into my face almost from between my feet, I saw, I could swear it—I felt it then, and know it now, the infernal gaze and the accursed countenance of my old friend in the portrait, transfused into the visage of the bloated vermin before me.

I bounced into my room again with a feeling of loathing and horror I cannot describe, and locked and bolted my door as if a lion had been at the other side. D—n him or it; curse the portrait and its original! I felt in my soul that the rat—yes, the rat, the

RAT I had just seen, was that evil being in masquerade, and rambling through the house upon some infernal night lark.

Next morning I was early trudging through the miry streets; and, among other transactions, posted a peremptory note recalling Tom. On my return, however, I found a note from my absent "chum," announcing his intended return next day. I was doubly rejoiced at this, because I had succeeded in getting rooms; and because the change of scene and return of my comrade were rendered specially pleasant by the last night's half ridiculous half horrible adventure.

I slept extemporaneously in my new quarters in Digges' Street that night, and next morning returned for breakfast to the haunted mansion, where I was certain Tom would call immediately on his arrival.

I was quite right—he came; and almost his first question referred to the primary object of our change of residence.

"Thank God," he said with genuine fervour, on hearing that all was arranged. "On your account I am delighted. As to myself, I assure you that no earthly consideration could have induced me ever again to pass a night in this disastrous old house."

"Confound the house!" I ejaculated, with a genuine mixture of fear and detestation, "we have not had a pleasant hour since we came to live here"; and so I went on, and related incidentally my adventure with the plethoric old rat.

"Well, if that were all," said my cousin, affecting to make light of the matter, "I don't think I should have minded it very much."

"Ay, but its eye—its countenance, my dear Tom," urged I; "if you had seen that, you would have felt it might be anything but what it seemed."

"I inclined to think the best conjurer in such a case would be an able-bodied cat," he said, with a provoking chuckle.

"But let us hear your own adventure," I said tartly.

At this challenge he looked uneasily round him. I had poked up a very unpleasant recollection.

"You shall hear it, Dick; I'll tell it to you," he said. "Begad, sir, I should feel quite queer, though, telling it here, though we are too strong a body for ghosts to meddle with just now."

Though he spoke this like a joke, I think it was serious calculation. Our Hebe was in a corner of the room, packing our cracked delft tea and dinner-services in a basket. She soon suspended operations, and with mouth and eyes wide open became an absorbed listener. Tom's experiences were told nearly in these words:----

"I saw it three times, Dick—three distinct times; and I am perfectly certain it meant me some infernal harm. I was, I say, in danger—in extreme danger; for, if nothing else had happened, my reason would most certainly have failed me, unless I had escaped so soon. Thank God. I did escape.

"The first night of this hateful disturbance, I was lying in the attitude of sleep, in that lumbering old bed. I hate to think of it. I was really wide awake, though I had put out my candle, and was lying as quietly as if I had been asleep; and although accidentally restless, my thoughts were running in a cheerful and agreeable channel.

"I think it must have been two o'clock at least when I thought I heard a sound in that—that odious dark recess at the far end of the bedroom. It was as if someone was drawing a piece of cord slowly along the floor, lifting it up, and dropping it softly down again in coils. I sate up once or twice in my bed, but could see nothing, so I concluded it must be mice in the wainscot. I felt no emotion graver than curiosity, and after a few minutes ceased to observe it.

"While lying in this state, strange to say; without at first a suspicion of anything supernatural, on a sudden I saw an old man, rather stout and square, in a sort of roan-red dressing-gown, and with a black cap on his head, moving stiffly and slowly in a diagonal direction, from the recess, across the floor of the bedroom, passing my bed at the foot, and entering the lumber-closet at the left. He had something under his arm; his head hung a little at one side; and, merciful God! when I saw his face."

Tom stopped for a while, and then said----

"That awful countenance, which living or dying I never can forget, disclosed what he was. Without turning to the right or left, he passed beside me, and entered the closet by the bed's head.

"While this fearful and indescribable type of death and guilt was passing, I felt that I had no more power to speak or stir than if I had been myself a corpse. For hours after it had disappeared, I was too terrified and weak to move. As soon as daylight came, I took courage, and examined the room, and especially the course which the frightful intruder had seemed to take, but there was not a vestige to indicate anybody's having passed there; no sign of any disturbing agency visible among the lumber that strewed the floor of the closet.

"I now began to recover a little. I was fagged and exhausted, and at last, overpowered by a feverish sleep. I came down late; and finding you out of spirits, on account of your dreams about the portrait, whose original I am now certain disclosed himself to me, I did not care to talk about the infernal vision. In fact, I was trying to persuade myself that the whole thing was an illusion, and I did not like to revive in their intensity the hated impressions of the past night—or to risk the constancy of my scepticism, by recounting the tale of my sufferings.

"It required some nerve, I can tell you, to go to my haunted chamber next night, and lie down quietly in the same bed," continued Tom. "I did so with a degree of trepidation, which, I am not ashamed to say, a very little matter would have sufficed to stimulate to downright panic. This night, however, passed off quietly enough, as also the next; and so too did two or three more. I grew more confident, and began to fancy that I believed in the theories of spectral illusions, with which I had at first vainly tried to impose upon my convictions.

"The apparition had been, indeed, altogether anomalous. It had crossed the room without any recognition of my presence: I had not disturbed it, and it had no mission to me. What, then, was the imaginable use of its crossing the room in a visible shape at all? Of course it might have been in the closet instead of going there, as easily as it introduced itself into the recess without entering the chamber in a shape discernible by the senses. Besides, how the deuce had I seen it? It was a dark night; I had no candle; there was no fire; and yet I saw it as distinctly, in colouring and outline, as ever I beheld human form! A cataleptic dream would explain it all; and I was determined that a dream it should be.

"One of the most remarkable phenomena connected with the practice of mendacity is the vast number of deliberate lies we tell ourselves, whom, of all persons, we can least expect to deceive. In all this, I need hardly tell you, Dick, I was simply lying to myself, and did not believe one word of the wretched humbug. Yet I went on, as men will do, like persevering charlatans and impostors, who tire people into credulity by the mere force of reiteration; so I hoped to win myself over at last to a comfortable scepticism about the ghost.

"He had not appeared a second time—that certainly was a comfort; and what, after all, did I care for him, and his queer old toggery and strange looks? Not a fig! I was nothing the worse for having seen him, and a good story the better. So I tumbled into bed, put out my candle, and, cheered by a loud drunken quarrel in the back lane, went fast asleep.

"From this deep slumber I awoke with a start. I knew I had had a horrible dream; but what it was I could not remember. My heart was thumping furiously; I felt bewildered and feverish; I sate up in the bed and looked about the room. A broad flood of moonlight came in through the curtainless window; everything was as I had last seen it; and though the domestic squabble in the back lane was, unhappily for me, allayed, I yet could hear a pleasant fellow singing, on his way home, the then popular comic ditty called, 'Murphy Delany.' Taking advantage of this diversion I lay down again, with my face towards the fireplace, and closing my eyes, did my best to think of nothing else but the song, which was every moment growing fainter in the distance:----

"'Twas Murphy Delany, so funny and frisky,

Stept into a shebeen shop to get his skin full;

He reeled out again pretty well lined with whiskey,

As fresh as a shamrock, as blind as a bull.

"The singer, whose condition I dare say resembled that of his hero, was soon too far off to regale my ears any more; and as his music died away, I myself sank into a doze, neither sound nor refreshing. Somehow the song had got into my head, and I went meandering on through the adventures of my respectable fellow-countryman, who, on emerging from the 'shebeen shop,' fell into a river, from which he was fished up to be 'sat upon' by a coroner's jury, who having learned from a 'horse-doctor' that he was 'dead as a door-nail, so there was an end,' returned their verdict accordingly, just as he returned to his senses, when an angry altercation and a pitched battle between the body and the coroner winds up the lay with due spirit and pleasantry.

"Through this ballad I continued with a weary monotony to plod, down to the very last line, and then da capo, and so on, in my uncomfortable half-sleep, for how long, I can't conjecture. I found myself at last, however, muttering, 'dead as a door-nail, so there was an end'; and something like another voice within me, seemed to say, very faintly, but sharply, 'dead! dead! dead! and may the Lord have mercy on your soul!' and instantaneously I was wide awake, and staring right before me from the pillow.

"Now—will you believe it, Dick?—I saw the same accursed figure standing full front, and gazing at me with its stony and fiendish countenance, not two yards from the bedside."

Tom stopped here, and wiped the perspiration from his face. I felt very queer. The girl was as pale as Tom; and, assembled as we were in the very scene of these adventures, we were all, I dare say, equally grateful for the clear daylight and the resuming bustle out of doors.

"For about three seconds only I saw it plainly; then it grew indistinct; but, for a long time, there was something like a column of dark vapour where it had been standing, between me and the wall; and I felt sure that he was still there. After a good while, this appearance went too. I took my clothes downstairs to the hall, and dressed there, with the door half open; then went out into the street, and walked about the town till morning, when I came back, in a miserable state of nervousness and exhaustion. I was such a fool, Dick, as to be ashamed to tell you how I came to be so upset. I thought you would laugh at me; especially as I had always talked philosophy, and treated your ghosts with contempt. I concluded you would give me no quarter; and so kept my tale of horror to myself.

"Now, Dick, you will hardly believe me, when I assure you, that for many nights after this last experience, I did not go to my room at all. I used to sit up for a while in the drawing-room after you had gone up to your bed; and then steal down softly to the hall-door, let myself out, and sit in the 'Robin Hood' tavern until the last guest went off; and then I got through the night like a sentry, pacing the streets till morning.

"For more than a week I never slept in bed. I sometimes had a snooze on a form in the 'Robin Hood,' and sometimes a nap in a chair during the day; but regular sleep I had absolutely none.

"I was quite resolved that we should get into another house; but I could not bring myself to tell you the reason, and I somehow put it off from day to day, although my life was, during every hour of this procrastination, rendered as miserable as that of a felon with the constables on his track. I was growing absolutely ill from this wretched mode of life.

"One afternoon I determined to enjoy an hour's sleep upon your bed. I hated mine; so that I had never, except in a stealthy visit every day to unmake it, lest Martha should discover the secret of my nightly absence, entered the ill-omened chamber.

"As ill-luck would have it, you had locked your bedroom, and taken away the key. I went into my own to unsettle the bedclothes, as usual, and give the bed the appearance of having been slept in. Now, a variety of circumstances concurred to bring about the dreadful scene through which I was that night to pass. In the first place, I was literally overpowered with fatigue, and longing for sleep; in the next place, the effect of this extreme exhaustion upon my nerves resembled that of a narcotic, and rendered me less susceptible than, perhaps, I should in any other condition have been, of the exciting fears which had become habitual to me. Then again, a little bit of the window was open, a pleasant freshness pervaded the room, and, to crown all, the cheerful sun of day was making the room quite pleasant. What was to prevent my enjoying an hour's nap here? The whole air was resonant with the cheerful hum of life, and the broad matter-of-fact light of day filled every corner of the room.

"I yielded—stifling my qualms—to the almost overpowering

temptation; and merely throwing off my coat, and loosening my cravat, I lay down, limiting myself to half-an-hour's doze in the unwonted enjoyment of a feather bed, a coverlet, and a bolster.

"It was horribly insidious; and the demon, no doubt, marked my infatuated preparations. Dolt that I was, I fancied, with mind and body worn out for want of sleep, and an arrear of a full week's rest to my credit, that such measure as half-an-hour's sleep, in such a situation, was possible. My sleep was death-like, long, and dreamless.

"Without a start or fearful sensation of any kind, I waked gently, but completely. It was, as you have good reason to remember, long past midnight—I believe, about two o'clock. When sleep has been deep and long enough to satisfy nature thoroughly, one often wakens in this way, suddenly, tranquilly, and completely.

"There was a figure seated in that lumbering, old sofa-chair, near the fireplace. Its back was rather towards me, but I could not be mistaken; it turned slowly round, and, merciful heavens! there was the stony face, with its infernal lineaments of malignity and despair, gloating on me. There was now no doubt as to its consciousness of my presence, and the hellish malice with which it was animated, for it arose, and drew close to the bedside. There was a rope about its neck, and the other end, coiled up, it held stiffly in its hand.

"My good angel nerved me for this horrible crisis. I remained for some seconds transfixed by the gaze of this tremendous phantom. He came close to the bed, and appeared on the point of mounting upon it. The next instant I was upon the floor at the far side, and in a moment more was, I don't know how, upon the lobby.

"But the spell was not yet broken; the valley of the shadow of death was not yet traversed. The abhorred phantom was before me there; it was standing near the banisters, stooping a little, and with one end of the rope round its own neck, was poising a noose at the other, as if to throw over mine; and while engaged in this baleful pantomime, it wore a smile so sensual, so unspeakably dreadful, that my senses were nearly overpowered. I saw and remember nothing more, until I found myself in your room.

"I had a wonderful escape, Dick—there is no disputing that—an escape for which, while I live, I shall bless the mercy of heaven. No one can conceive or imagine what it is for flesh and blood to stand in the presence of such a thing, but one who has had the terrific experience. Dick, Dick, a shadow has passed over me—a chill has crossed my blood and marrow, and I will never be the same again—never, Dick—never!"

Our handmaid, a mature girl of two-and-fifty, as I have said, stayed her hand, as Tom's story proceeded, and by little and little drew near to us, with open mouth, and her brows contracted over her little, beady black eyes, till stealing a glance over her shoulder now and then, she established herself close behind us. During the relation, she had made various earnest comments, in an undertone; but these and her ejaculations, for the sake of brevity and simplicity, I have omitted in my narration.

"It's often I heard tell of it," she now said, "but I never believed it rightly till now—though, indeed, why should not I? Does not my mother, down there in the lane, know quare stories, God bless us, beyant telling about it? But you ought not to have slept in the back bedroom. She was loath to let me be going in and out of that room even in the day time, let alone for any Christian to spend the night in it; for sure she says it was his own bedroom."

"Whose own bedroom?" we asked, in a breath.

"Why, his—the ould Judge's—Judge Horrock's, to be sure, God rest his sowl"; and she looked fearfully round.

"Amen!" I muttered. "But did he die there?"

"Die there! No, not quite there," she said. "Shure, was not it over the banisters he hung himself, the ould sinner, God be merciful to us all? and was not it in the alcove they found the handles of the skipping-rope cut off, and the knife where he was settling the cord, God bless us, to hang himself with? It was his housekeeper's daughter owned the rope, my mother often told me, and the child never throve after, and used to be starting up out of her sleep, and screeching in the night time, wid dhrames and frights that cum an her; and they said how it was the speerit of the ould Judge that was tormentin' her; and she used to be roaring and yelling out to hould back the big ould fellow with the crooked neck; and then she'd screech 'Oh, the master! the master! he's stampin' at me, and beckoning to me! Mother, darling, don't let me go!' And so the poor crathure died at last, and the docthers said it was wather on the brain, for it was all they could say."

"How long ago was all this?" I asked.

"Oh, then, how would I know?" she answered. "But it must be a wondherful long time ago, for the housekeeper was an ould woman, with a pipe in her mouth, and not a tooth left, and better nor eighty years ould when my mother was first married; and they said she was a rale buxom, fine-dressed woman when the ould Judge come to his end; an', indeed, my mother's not far from eighty years ould herself this day; and what made it worse for the unnatural ould villain, God rest his soul, to frighten the little girl out of the world the way he did, was what was mostly thought and believed by every one. My mother says how the poor little crathure was his own child; for he was by all accounts an ould villain every way, an' the hangin'est judge that ever was known in Ireland's ground."

"From what you said about the danger of sleeping in that bedroom," said I, "I suppose there were stories about the ghost having appeared there to others."

"Well, there was things said—quare things, surely," she

answered, as it seemed, with some reluctance. "And why would not there? Sure was it not up in that same room he slept for more than twenty years? and was it not in the alcove he got the rope ready that done his own business at last, the way he done many a betther man's in his lifetime?—and was not the body lying in the same bed after death, and put in the coffin there, too, and carried out to his grave from it in Pether's churchyard, after the coroner was done? But there was quare stories—my mother has them all —about how one Nicholas Spaight got into trouble on the head of it."

"And what did they say of this Nicholas Spaight?" I asked.

"Oh, for that matther, it's soon told," she answered.

And she certainly did relate a very strange story, which so piqued my curiosity, that I took occasion to visit the ancient lady, her mother, from whom I learned many very curious particulars. Indeed, I am tempted to tell the tale, but my fingers are weary, and I must defer it. But if you wish to hear it another time, I shall do my best.

When we had heard the strange tale I have not told you, we put one or two further questions to her about the alleged spectral visitations, to which the house had, ever since the death of the wicked old Judge, been subjected.

"No one ever had luck in it," she told us. "There was always cross accidents, sudden deaths, and short times in it. The first that tuck, it was a family—I forget their name—but at any rate there was two young ladies and their papa. He was about sixty, and a stout healthy gentleman as you'd wish to see at that age. Well, he slept in that unlucky back bedroom; and, God between us an' harm! sure enough he was found dead one morning, half out of the bed, with his head as black as a sloe, and swelled like a puddin', hanging down near the floor. It was a fit, they said. He was as dead as a mackerel, and so he could not say what it was; but the ould people was all sure that it was nothing at all but the ould Judge, God bless us! that frightened him out of his senses and his life together.

"Some time after there was a rich old maiden lady took the house. I don't know which room she slept in, but she lived alone; and at any rate, one morning, the servants going down early to their work, found her sitting on the passage-stairs, shivering and talkin' to herself, quite mad; and never a word more could any of them or her friends get from her ever afterwards but, 'Don't ask me to go, for I promised to wait for him.' They never made out from her who it was she meant by him, but of course those that knew all about the ould house were at no loss for the meaning of all that happened to her.

"Then afterwards, when the house was let out in lodgings, there was Micky Byrne that took the same room, with his wife and three little children; and sure I heard Mrs. Byrne myself telling how the children used to be lifted up in the bed at night, she could not see by what mains; and how they were starting and screeching every hour, just all as one as the housekeeper's little girl that died, till at last one night poor Micky had a dhrop in him, the way he used now and again; and what do you think in the middle of the night he thought he heard a noise on the stairs, and being in liquor, nothing less id do him but out he must go himself to see what was wrong. Well, after that, all she ever heard of him was himself sayin', 'Oh, God!' and a tumble that shook the very house; and there, sure enough, he was lying on the lower stairs, under the lobby, with his neck smashed double undher him, where he was flung over the banisters."

Then the handmaiden added----

"I'll go down to the lane, and send up Joe Gavvey to pack up the rest of the taythings, and bring all the things across to your new lodgings."

And so we all sallied out together, each of us breathing more freely, I have no doubt, as we crossed that ill-omened threshold for the last time.

Now, I may add thus much, in compliance with the immemorial usage of the realm of fiction, which sees the hero not only through his adventures, but fairly out of the world. You must have perceived that what the flesh, blood, and bone hero of romance proper is to the regular compounder of fiction, this old house of brick, wood, and mortar is to the humble recorder of this true tale. I, therefore, relate, as in duty bound, the catastrophe which ultimately befell it, which was simply this—that about two years subsequently to my story it was taken by a quack doctor, who called himself Baron Duhlstoerf, and filled the parlour windows with bottles of indescribable horrors preserved in brandy, and the newspapers with the usual grandiloquent and mendacious advertisements. This gentleman among his virtues did not reckon sobriety, and one night, being overcome with much wine, he set fire to his bed curtains, partially burned himself, and totally consumed the house. It was afterwards rebuilt, and for a time an undertaker established himself in the premises.

I have now told you my own and Tom's adventures, together with some valuable collateral particulars; and having acquitted myself of my engagement, I wish you a very good night, and pleasant dreams.

THE RED NOSED REINDEER

By Marcus Helms

A reminder now in a short story from American author Marcus Helms why it is very important to stay off Santa's naughty list.

THE RED NOSED REINDEER

The harsh winter wind sweeps through the farm, rattling the wooden doors to an old barnyard like an angry soul trying to get in. Hidden by thick trees, two sea green eyes peer through the darkness. Watching. Waiting.

A soft hand comes up to wipe a tear meandering its way down Lena's supple cheek. At only 16 years old, 5 ft 2 and fiery red bangs, Lena is the last person you would assume to be hiding in the dark with a butcher's knife clutched in her hand. A life will be taken tonight.

Head on a swivel, Lena creeps towards the barnyard, her footsteps crunching fresh snow underneath her soles. It is now or never, all that she has on her side is the element of surprise but her victim won't go down without a fight.

As Lena moves closer to the barnyard, her mind races with memories of her brother, Rudolf. She remembers how he used to point at her freckles and call them her little constellation, she in turn would mock him for his eternally red nose, an outcome of their Scottish heritage and another reminder to her of the bond they share.

We all know Father Christmas has flying reindeer but we never think to question how or why. Lena knows why, she knows only too well. The rumours of his experiments on humans are true, and they have gone far beyond his army of mindless grinning slaves that he refers to as his 'jolly little elves' with his creepy Ho, Ho, Ho.

Lena has found something darker, a chimaera, she knows now what happened to her brother when Santa placed him on his naughty list.

Steeling herself, Lena presses her thumb into the blade of the knife taking power from the pain it causes, she loves her brother more than anything in this world; tonight she will free him, one way or another.

BOOM! - Lena kicks in the barnyard doors, butcher's knife held high; death will happen tonight.

THE SIGNAL MAN

By Charles Dickens

"The Signal Man" by Charles Dickens is not explicitly a Christmas story. Unlike some of Dickens's other famous works, such as "A Christmas Carol", "The Signal Man" does not centre around the theme of Christmas or the holiday season. However, as I deeply love the tale and indeed first came across it at a fireside reading of Christmas ghost stories, I am claiming its inclusion here by dint of its first publication in the extra Christmas edition of Dickens's magazine, All the Year Round in 1866.

THE SIGNAL MAN

"Halloa! Below there!"

When he heard a voice thus calling to him, he was standing at the door of his box, with a flag in his hand, furled round its short pole. One would have thought, considering the nature of the ground, that he could not have doubted from what quarter the voice came; but instead of looking up to where I stood on the top of the steep cutting nearly over his head, he turned himself about, and looked down the Line. There was something remarkable in his manner of doing so, though I could not have said for my life what. But I know it was remarkable enough to attract my notice, even though his figure was foreshortened and shadowed, down in the deep trench, and mine was high above him, so steeped in the glow of an angry sunset, that I had shaded my eyes with my hand before I saw him at all.

"Halloa! Below!"

From looking down the Line, he turned himself about again, and, raising his eyes, saw my figure high above him.

"Is there any path by which I can come down and speak to you?"

He looked up at me without replying, and I looked down at him without pressing him too soon with a repetition of my idle question. Just then there came a vague vibration in the earth and air, quickly changing into a violent pulsation, and an oncoming rush that caused me to start back, as though it had force to draw me down. When such vapour as rose to my height from this rapid train had passed me, and was skimming away over the landscape, I looked down again, and saw him refurling the flag he had shown while the train went by.

I repeated my inquiry. After a pause, during which he seemed to regard me with fixed attention, he motioned with his rolled-up flag towards a point on my level, some two or three hundred yards distant. I called down to him, "All right!" and made for that point. There, by dint of looking closely about me, I found a rough zigzag descending path notched out, which I followed.

The cutting was extremely deep, and unusually precipitate. It was made through a clammy stone, that became oozier and wetter as I went down. For these reasons, I found the way long enough to give me time to recall a singular air of reluctance or compulsion with which he had pointed out the path.

When I came down low enough upon the zigzag descent to see him again, I saw that he was standing between the rails on the way by which the train had lately passed, in an attitude as if he were waiting for me to appear. He had his left hand at his chin, and that left elbow rested on his right hand, crossed over his breast. His attitude was one of such expectation and watchfulness that I stopped a moment, wondering at it.

I resumed my downward way, and stepping out upon the level of the railroad, and drawing nearer to him, saw that he was a dark sallow man, with a dark beard and rather heavy eyebrows. His post was in as solitary and dismal a place as ever I saw. On either side, a dripping-wet wall of jagged stone, excluding all view but a strip of sky; the perspective one way only a crooked prolongation of this great dungeon; the shorter perspective in the other direction terminating in a gloomy red light, and the gloomier entrance to a black tunnel, in whose massive architecture there was a barbarous, depressing, and forbidding air. So little sunlight ever found its way to this spot, that it had an earthy, deadly smell; and so much cold wind rushed through it, that it struck chill to me, as if I had left the natural world.

Before he stirred, I was near enough to him to have touched him.

Not even then removing his eyes from mine, he stepped back one step, and lifted his hand.

This was a lonesome post to occupy (I said), and it had riveted my attention when I looked down from up yonder. A visitor was a rarity, I should suppose; not an unwelcome rarity, I hoped? In me, he merely saw a man who had been shut up within narrow limits all his life, and who, being at last set free, had a newly-awakened interest in these great works. To such purpose I spoke to him; but I am far from sure of the terms I used; for, besides that I am not happy in opening any conversation, there was something in the man that daunted me.

He directed a most curious look towards the red light near the tunnel's mouth, and looked all about it, as if something were missing from it, and then looked it me.

That light was part of his charge? Was it not?

He answered in a low voice,—"Don't you know it is?"

The monstrous thought came into my mind, as I perused the fixed eyes and the saturnine face, that this was a spirit, not a man. I have speculated since, whether there may have been infection in his mind.

In my turn, I stepped back. But in making the action, I detected in his eyes some latent fear of me. This put the monstrous thought to flight.

"You look at me," I said, forcing a smile, "as if you had a dread of me."

"I was doubtful," he returned, "whether I had seen you before."

"Where?"

He pointed to the red light he had looked at.

"There?" I said.

Intently watchful of me, he replied (but without sound), "Yes."

"My good fellow, what should I do there? However, be that as it may, I never was there, you may swear."

"I think I may," he rejoined. "Yes; I am sure I may."

His manner cleared, like my own. He replied to my remarks with readiness, and in well-chosen words. Had he much to do there? Yes; that was to say, he had enough responsibility to bear; but exactness and watchfulness were what was required of him, and of actual work— manual labour—he had next to none. To change that signal, to trim those lights, and to turn this iron handle now and then, was all he had to do under that head. Regarding those many long and lonely hours of which I seemed to make so much, he could only say that the routine of his life had shaped itself into that form, and he had grown used to it. He had taught himself a language down here,—if only to know it by sight, and to have formed his own crude ideas of its pronunciation, could be called learning it. He had also worked at fractions and decimals, and tried a little algebra; but he was, and had been as a boy, a poor hand at figures. Was it necessary for him when on duty always to remain in that channel of damp air, and could he never rise into the sunshine from between those high stone walls? Why, that depended upon times and circumstances. Under some conditions there would be less upon the Line than under others, and the same held good as to certain hours of the day and night. In bright weather, he did choose occasions for getting a little above these lower shadows; but, being at all times liable to be called by his electric bell, and at such times listening for it with redoubled anxiety, the relief was less than I would suppose.

He took me into his box, where there was a fire, a desk for an official book in which he had to make certain entries, a telegraphic instrument with its dial, face, and needles, and the little bell of which he had spoken. On my trusting that he would excuse the remark that he had been well educated, and (I hoped I might say without offence) perhaps educated above that station, he observed that instances of slight incongruity in such wise would rarely be found wanting among large bodies of men; that he had heard it was so in workhouses, in the police force, even in that last desperate resource, the army; and that he knew it was so, more or less, in any great railway staff. He had been, when young (if I could believe it, sitting in that hut,—he scarcely could), a student of natural philosophy, and had attended lectures; but he had run wild, misused his opportunities, gone down, and never risen again. He had no complaint to offer about that. He had made his bed, and he lay upon it. It was far too late to make another.

All that I have here condensed he said in a quiet manner, with his grave dark regards divided between me and the fire. He threw in the word, "Sir," from time to time, and especially when he referred to his youth,—as though to request me to understand that he claimed to be nothing but what I found him. He was several times interrupted by the little bell, and had to read off messages, and send replies. Once he had to stand without the door, and display a flag as a train passed, and make some verbal communication to the driver. In the discharge of his duties, I observed him to be remarkably exact and vigilant, breaking off his discourse at a syllable, and remaining silent until what he had to do was done.

In a word, I should have set this man down as one of the safest of men to be employed in that capacity, but for the circumstance that while he was speaking to me he twice broke off with a fallen colour, turned his face towards the little bell when it did not ring, opened the door of the hut (which was kept shut to exclude the unhealthy damp), and looked out towards the red light near the mouth of the tunnel. On both of those occasions, he came back to the fire with the inexplicable air upon him which I had remarked, without being able to define, when we were so far asunder.

Said I, when I rose to leave him, “You almost make me think that I have met with a contented man.”

(I am afraid I must acknowledge that I said it to lead him on.)

“I believe I used to be so,” he rejoined, in the low voice in which he had first spoken; “but I am troubled, sir, I am troubled.”

He would have recalled the words if he could. He had said them, however, and I took them up quickly.

“With what? What is your trouble?”

“It is very difficult to impart, sir. It is very, very difficult to speak of. If ever you make me another visit, I will try to tell you.”

“But I expressly intend to make you another visit. Say, when shall it be?”

“I go off early in the morning, and I shall be on again at ten to-morrow night, sir.”

“I will come at eleven.”

He thanked me, and went out at the door with me. “I’ll show my white light, sir,” he said, in his peculiar low voice, “till you have found the way up. When you have found it, don’t call out! And when you are at the top, don’t call out!”

His manner seemed to make the place strike colder to me, but I said no more than, “Very well.”

“And when you come down to-morrow night, don’t call out! Let me ask you a parting question. What made you cry, ‘Halloa! Below there!’ to-night?”

“Heaven knows,” said I. “I cried something to that effect—”

“Not to that effect, sir. Those were the very words. I know them well.”

"Admit those were the very words. I said them, no doubt, because I saw you below."

"For no other reason?"

"What other reason could I possibly have?"

"You had no feeling that they were conveyed to you in any supernatural way?"

"No."

He wished me good-night, and held up his light. I walked by the side of the down Line of rails (with a very disagreeable sensation of a train coming behind me) until I found the path. It was easier to mount than to descend, and I got back to my inn without any adventure.

Punctual to my appointment, I placed my foot on the first notch of the zigzag next night, as the distant clocks were striking eleven. He was waiting for me at the bottom, with his white light on. "I have not called out," I said, when we came close together; "may I speak now?" "By all means, sir." "Good-night, then, and here's my hand." "Good-night, sir, and here's mine." With that we walked side by side to his box, entered it, closed the door, and sat down by the fire.

"I have made up my mind, sir," he began, bending forward as soon as we were seated, and speaking in a tone but a little above a whisper, "that you shall not have to ask me twice what troubles me. I took you for some one else yesterday evening. That troubles me."

"That mistake?"

"No. That some one else."

"Who is it?"

"I don't know."

"Like me?"

"I don't know. I never saw the face. The left arm is across the face, and the right arm is waved,—violently waved. This way."

I followed his action with my eyes, and it was the action of an arm gesticulating, with the utmost passion and vehemence, "For God's sake, clear the way!"

"One moonlight night," said the man, "I was sitting here, when I heard a voice cry, 'Halloa! Below there!' I started up, looked from that door, and saw this Some one else standing by the red light near the tunnel, waving as I just now showed you. The voice seemed hoarse with shouting, and it cried, 'Look out! Look out!' And then again, 'Halloa! Below there! Look out!' I caught up my lamp, turned it on red, and ran towards the figure, calling, 'What's wrong? What has happened? Where?' It stood just outside the blackness of the tunnel. I advanced so close upon it that I wondered at its keeping the sleeve across its eyes. I ran right up at it, and had my hand stretched out to pull the sleeve away, when it was gone."

"Into the tunnel?" said I.

"No. I ran on into the tunnel, five hundred yards. I stopped, and held my lamp above my head, and saw the figures of the measured distance, and saw the wet stains stealing down the walls and trickling through the arch. I ran out again faster than I had run in (for I had a mortal abhorrence of the place upon me), and I looked all round the red light with my own red light, and I went up the iron ladder to the gallery atop of it, and I came down again, and ran back here. I telegraphed both ways, 'An alarm has been given. Is anything wrong?' The answer came back, both ways, 'All well.'"

Resisting the slow touch of a frozen finger tracing out my spine, I showed him how that this figure must be a deception of his sense of sight; and how that figures, originating in disease of the delicate nerves that minister to the functions of the eye, were known to have often troubled patients, some of whom had become conscious of the nature of their affliction, and had even proved it by experiments upon themselves. "As to an imaginary cry," said I, "do but listen for a moment to the wind in this unnatural valley while we speak so low, and to the wild harp it makes of the telegraph wires."

That was all very well, he returned, after we had sat listening for a while, and he ought to know something of the wind and the wires,— he who so often passed long winter nights there, alone and watching. But he would beg to remark that he had not finished.

I asked his pardon, and he slowly added these words, touching my arm, -

"Within six hours after the Appearance, the memorable accident on this Line happened, and within ten hours the dead and wounded were brought along through the tunnel over the spot where the figure had stood."

A disagreeable shudder crept over me, but I did my best against it. It was not to be denied, I rejoined, that this was a remarkable coincidence, calculated deeply to impress his mind. But it was unquestionable that remarkable coincidences did continually occur, and they must be taken into account in dealing with such a subject. Though to be sure I must admit, I added (for I thought I saw that he was going to bring the objection to bear upon me), men of common sense did not allow much for coincidences in making the ordinary calculations of life.

He again begged to remark that he had not finished.

I again begged his pardon for being betrayed into interruptions.

"This," he said, again laying his hand upon my arm, and glancing over his shoulder with hollow eyes, "was just a year ago. Six or seven months passed, and I had recovered from the surprise and shock, when one morning, as the day was breaking, I, standing at the door, looked towards the red light, and saw the spectre again." He stopped, with a fixed look at me.

"Did it cry out?"

"No. It was silent."

"Did it wave its arm?"

"No. It leaned against the shaft of the light, with both hands before the face. Like this."

Once more I followed his action with my eyes. It was an action of mourning. I have seen such an attitude in stone figures on tombs.

"Did you go up to it?"

"I came in and sat down, partly to collect my thoughts, partly because it had turned me faint. When I went to the door again, daylight was above me, and the ghost was gone."

"But nothing followed? Nothing came of this?"

He touched me on the arm with his forefinger twice or thrice giving a ghastly nod each time:-

"That very day, as a train came out of the tunnel, I noticed, at a carriage window on my side, what looked like a confusion of hands and heads, and something waved. I saw it just in time to signal the driver, Stop! He shut off, and put his brake on, but the train drifted past here a hundred and fifty yards or more. I ran after it, and, as I went along, heard terrible screams and cries. A beautiful young lady had died instantaneously in one of the compartments, and was brought in here, and laid down on this floor between us."

Involuntarily I pushed my chair back, as I looked from the boards at which he pointed to himself.

"True, sir. True. Precisely as it happened, so I tell it you."

I could think of nothing to say, to any purpose, and my mouth was very dry. The wind and the wires took up the story with a long lamenting wail.

He resumed. "Now, sir, mark this, and judge how my mind is troubled. The spectre came back a week ago. Ever since, it has been there, now and again, by fits and starts."

"At the light?"

"At the Danger-light."

"What does it seem to do?"

He repeated, if possible with increased passion and vehemence, that former gesticulation of, "For God's sake, clear the way!"

Then he went on. "I have no peace or rest for it. It calls to me, for many minutes together, in an agonised manner, 'Below there! Look out! Look out!' It stands waving to me. It rings my little bell —"

I caught at that. "Did it ring your bell yesterday evening when I was here, and you went to the door?"

"Twice."

"Why, see," said I, "how your imagination misleads you. My eyes were on the bell, and my ears were open to the bell, and if I am a living man, it did not ring at those times. No, nor at any other time, except when it was rung in the natural course of physical things by the station communicating with you."

He shook his head. "I have never made a mistake as to that yet, sir. I have never confused the spectre's ring with the man's. The ghost's ring is a strange vibration in the bell that it derives from nothing else, and I have not asserted that the bell stirs to the eye. I don't wonder that you failed to hear it. But I heard it."

"And did the spectre seem to be there, when you looked out?"

"It was there."'

"Both times?"

He repeated firmly: "Both times."

"Will you come to the door with me, and look for it now?"

He bit his under lip as though he were somewhat unwilling, but arose. I opened the door, and stood on the step, while he stood in the doorway. There was the Danger-light. There was the dismal mouth of the tunnel. There were the high, wet stone walls of the cutting. There were the stars above them.

"Do you see it?" I asked him, taking particular note of his face. His eyes were prominent and strained, but not very much more so, perhaps, than my own had been when I had directed them earnestly towards the same spot.

"No," he answered. "It is not there."

"Agreed," said I.

We went in again, shut the door, and resumed our seats. I was thinking how best to improve this advantage, if it might be called one, when he took up the conversation in such a matter-of-course way, so assuming that there could be no serious question of fact between us, that I felt myself placed in the weakest of positions.

"By this time you will fully understand, sir," he said, "that what troubles me so dreadfully is the question, What does the spectre mean?"

I was not sure, I told him, that I did fully understand.

"What is its warning against?" he said, ruminating, with his eyes on the fire, and only by times turning them on me. "What is the danger? Where is the danger? There is danger overhanging somewhere on the Line. Some dreadful calamity will happen. It is not to be doubted this third time, after what has gone before. But surely this is a cruel haunting of me. What can I do?"

He pulled out his handkerchief, and wiped the drops from his heated forehead.

"If I telegraph Danger, on either side of me, or on both, I can give no reason for it," he went on, wiping the palms of his hands. "I should get into trouble, and do no good. They would think I was mad. This is the way it would work,—Message: 'Danger! Take care!' Answer: 'What Danger? Where?' Message: 'Don't know. But, for God's sake, take care!' They would displace me. What else could they do?"

His pain of mind was most pitiable to see. It was the mental torture of a conscientious man, oppressed beyond endurance by an unintelligible responsibility involving life.

"When it first stood under the Danger-light," he went on, putting his dark hair back from his head, and drawing his hands outward across and across his temples in an extremity of feverish distress, "why not tell me where that accident was to happen,—if it must happen? Why not tell me how it could be averted,—if it could have been averted? When on its second coming it hid its face, why not tell me, instead, 'She is going to die. Let them keep her at home'? If it came, on those two occasions, only to show me that its warnings were true, and so to prepare me for the third, why not warn me plainly now? And I, Lord help me! A mere poor signal-man on this solitary station! Why not go to somebody with credit to be believed, and power to act?"

When I saw him in this state, I saw that for the poor man's sake, as well as for the public safety, what I had to do for the time was to compose his mind. Therefore, setting aside all question of reality or unreality between us, I represented to him that whoever thoroughly discharged his duty must do well, and that at least it was his comfort that he understood his duty, though he did not understand these confounding Appearances. In this effort I succeeded far better than in the attempt to reason him out of his conviction. He became calm; the occupations incidental to his post as the night advanced began to make larger demands on his attention: and I left him at two in the morning. I had offered to stay through the night, but he would not hear of it.

That I more than once looked back at the red light as I ascended the pathway, that I did not like the red light, and that I should have slept but poorly if my bed had been under it, I see no reason to conceal. Nor did I like the two sequences of the accident and the dead girl. I see no reason to conceal that either.

But what ran most in my thoughts was the consideration how ought I to act, having become the recipient of this disclosure? I had proved the man to be intelligent, vigilant, painstaking, and exact; but how long might he remain so, in his state of mind? Though in a subordinate position, still he held a most important trust, and would I (for instance) like to stake my own life on the chances of his continuing to execute it with precision?

Unable to overcome a feeling that there would be something treacherous in my communicating what he had told me to his superiors in the Company, without first being plain with himself and proposing a middle course to him, I ultimately resolved to offer to accompany him (otherwise keeping his secret for the present) to the wisest medical practitioner we could hear of in those parts, and to take his opinion. A change in his time of duty would come round next night, he had apprised me, and he would be off an hour or two after sunrise, and on again soon after sunset. I had appointed to return accordingly.

Next evening was a lovely evening, and I walked out early to enjoy it. The sun was not yet quite down when I traversed the field-path near the top of the deep cutting. I would extend my walk for an hour, I said to myself, half an hour on and half an hour back, and it would then be time to go to my signal-man's box.

Before pursuing my stroll, I stepped to the brink, and mechanically looked down, from the point from which I had first seen him. I cannot describe the thrill that seized upon me, when, close at the mouth of the tunnel, I saw the appearance of a man, with his left sleeve across his eyes, passionately waving his right arm.

The nameless horror that oppressed me passed in a moment, for in a moment I saw that this appearance of a man was a man indeed, and that there was a little group of other men, standing at a short distance, to whom he seemed to be rehearsing the gesture he made. The Danger-light was not yet lighted. Against its shaft, a little low hut, entirely new to me, had been made of some wooden supports and tarpaulin. It looked no bigger than a bed.

With an irresistible sense that something was wrong,—with a flashing self-reproachful fear that fatal mischief had come of my leaving the man there, and causing no one to be sent to overlook or correct what he did,—I descended the notched path with all the speed I could make.

"What is the matter?" I asked the men.

"Signal-man killed this morning, sir."

"Not the man belonging to that box?"

"Yes, sir."

"Not the man I know?"

"You will recognise him, sir, if you knew him," said the man who spoke for the others, solemnly uncovering his own head, and raising an end of the tarpaulin, "for his face is quite composed."

"O, how did this happen, how did this happen?" I asked, turning from one to another as the hut closed in again.

"He was cut down by an engine, sir. No man in England knew his work better. But somehow he was not clear of the outer rail. It was just at broad day. He had struck the light, and had the lamp in his hand. As the engine came out of the tunnel, his back was towards her, and she cut him down. That man drove her, and was showing how it happened. Show the gentleman, Tom."

The man, who wore a rough dark dress, stepped back to his former place at the mouth of the tunnel.

"Coming round the curve in the tunnel, sir," he said, "I saw him at the end, like as if I saw him down a perspective-glass. There was no time to check speed, and I knew him to be very careful. As he didn't seem to take heed of the whistle, I shut it off when we were running down upon him, and called to him as loud as I could call."

"What did you say?"

"I said, 'Below there! Look out! Look out! For God's sake, clear the way!'"

I started.

"Ah! it was a dreadful time, sir. I never left off calling to him. I put this arm before my eyes not to see, and I waved this arm to the last; but it was no use."

Without prolonging the narrative to dwell on any one of its curious circumstances more than on any other, I may, in closing it, point out the coincidence that the warning of the Engine-Driver included, not only the words which the unfortunate Signal-man had repeated to me as haunting him, but also the words which I myself—not he—had attached, and that only in my own mind, to the gesticulation he had imitated.

UNWRAPPING

By Evelyn Jones

I love a gift at Christmas, and you can enjoy the anticipation of this one with this debut short story from Australian author Evelyn Jones. I look forward with trepidation to seeing what gifts Evelyn has for us in the future...

UNWRAPPING

Audrey couldn't contain her excitement, as she saw the neatly wrapped Christmas present. Christmas had always been her favourite holiday, but since getting married to Mike, she'd had to somewhat temper it. Mike had other qualities that she loved, but if she were going to be honest, his lack of enthusiasm for Christmas and spontaneity had almost been a deal-breaker.

So, for him to wake up early on Christmas morning and lead her downstairs to present a beautifully wrapped box was unprecedented. Her heart beat with anticipation as Audrey slowly began to unwrap it, she felt a little guilty for how much she'd doubted Mike. Maybe there were layers to him that she had previously unseen, maybe he could actually be as exciting as her ex, Luke that she'd often find herself thinking about.

Mike watched her with a steady grin, a cup of his beloved coffee in his hands—black, 2 sugars, a little bit of cream. Audrey's hands trembled slightly as she continued to peel away the layers of wrapping paper. What could be so special about this gift that had him so giddy this Christmas morning?

Audrey finally reached the last layer of wrapping, her fingertips grazing the mysterious box beneath. She held her breath, it was very heavy, he had put so much care and attention into its presentation, what could it be? Her imagination ran wild with possibilities.

The room seemed to grow quieter as she carefully removed the final layer. Her eyes were fixed on Mike, his anticipation mirroring her own, he'd been waiting for this moment for a long time.

Audrey popped open the top of the box, looked inside, and released a scream that could strip paint from the walls. She doubled back to the wall, her eyes wide, her breath throttled.

Her eyes met Mike's, trying to read his next move, but Mike sat there calmly as if this was just another Tuesday. He brought the coffee to his mouth, paused, and uttered... "Merry Christmas." The chill of his words broke her. Audrey collapsed to her knees, looking one last time to the box.

Audrey's mind whirled with shock and terror, and the room seemed to close in around her as she looked into the cold dead eyes of Luke; maybe the affair wasn't the secret she thought it was.

THE CHRISTMAS BANQUET

By Nathaniel Hawthorne

"The Christmas Banquet" by Nathaniel Hawthorne was first published in 1844, The banquet mentioned in the title is an annual feast in which the ten most miserable individuals who can be found are gathered together for the holiday. Each year the guests chosen are different, but Gervaise Hastings, a man unafflicted by any obvious misfortune, is included year after year.

As an aside, Nathaniel Hawthorne's ancestor, John Hathorne, was a judge involved in the Salem Witch Trials in the late 17th century. Hathorne was notably harsh in his judgments and was the only judge involved who never repented of his actions. To attempt to distance himself from this ancestry, Hawthorne added a "w" to his surname.

THE CHRISTMAS BANQUET

"I have here attempted," said Roderick, unfolding a few sheets of manuscript, as he sat with Rosina and the sculptor in the summer-house,—"I have attempted to seize hold of a personage who glides past me, occasionally, in my walk through life. My former sad experience, as you know, has gifted me with some degree of insight into the gloomy mysteries of the human heart, through which I have wandered like one astray in a dark cavern, with his torch fast flickering to extinction. But this man, this class of men, is a hopeless puzzle."

"Well, but propound him," said the sculptor. "Let us have an idea of hint, to begin with."

"Why, indeed," replied Roderick, "he is such a being as I could conceive you to carve out of marble, and some yet unrealized perfection of human science to endow with an exquisite mockery of intellect; but still there lacks the last inestimable touch of a divine Creator. He looks like a man; and, perchance, like a better specimen of man than you ordinarily meet. You might esteem him wise; he is capable of cultivation and refinement, and has at least an external conscience; but the demands that spirit makes upon spirit are precisely those to which he cannot respond. When at last you come close to him you find him chill and unsubstantial,—a mere vapor."

"I believe," said Rosina, "I have a glimmering idea of what you mean."

"Then be thankful," answered her husband, smiling; "but do not anticipate any further illumination from what I am about to read. I have here imagined such a man to be—what, probably, he never is—conscious of the deficiency in his spiritual organization. Methinks the result would be a sense of cold unreality wherewith he would go shivering through the world, longing to exchange his load of ice for any burden of real grief that fate could fling upon a human being."

Contenting himself with this preface, Roderick began to read.

In a certain old gentleman's last will and testament there appeared a bequest, which, as his final thought and deed, was singularly in keeping with a long life of melancholy eccentricity. He devised a considerable sum for establishing a fund, the interest of which was to be expended, annually forever, in preparing a Christmas Banquet for ten of the most miserable persons that could be found. It seemed not to be the testator's purpose to make these half a score of sad hearts merry, but to provide that the stern or fierce expression of human discontent should not be drowned, even for that one holy and joyful day, amid the acclamations of festal gratitude which all Christendom sends up. And he desired, likewise, to perpetuate his own remonstrance against the earthly course of Providence, and his sad and sour dissent from those systems of religion or philosophy which either find sunshine in the world or draw it down from heaven.

The task of inviting the guests, or of selecting among such as might advance their claims to partake of this dismal hospitality, was confided to the two trustees or stewards of the fund. These gentlemen, like their deceased friend, were sombre humorists, who made it their principal occupation to number the sable threads in the web of human life, and drop all the golden ones out of the reckoning. They performed their present office with integrity and judgment. The aspect of the assembled company, on the day of the first festival, might not, it is true, have satisfied every beholder that these were especially the individuals, chosen forth from all the world, whose griefs were worthy to stand as indicators of the mass of human suffering.

Yet, after due consideration, it could not be disputed that here was a variety of hopeless discomfort, which, if it sometimes arose from causes apparently inadequate, was thereby only the shrewder imputation against the nature and mechanism of life.

The arrangements and decorations of the banquet were probably intended to signify that death in life which had been the testator's definition of existence. The hall, illuminated by torches, was hung round with curtains of deep and dusky purple, and adorned with branches of cypress and wreaths of artificial flowers, imitative of such as used to be strewn over the dead. A sprig of parsley was laid by every plate. The main reservoir of wine, was a sepulchral urn of silver, whence the liquor was distributed around the table in small vases, accurately copied from those that held the tears of ancient mourners. Neither had the stewards—if it were their taste that arranged these details—forgotten the fantasy of the old Egyptians, who seated a skeleton at every festive board, and mocked their own merriment with the imperturbable grin of a death's-head. Such a fearful guest, shrouded in a black mantle, sat now at the head of the table. It was whispered, I know not with what truth, that the testator himself had once walked the visible world with the machinery of that sane skeleton, and that it was one of the stipulations of his will, that he should thus be permitted to sit, from year to year, at the banquet which he had instituted. If so, it was perhaps covertly implied that he had cherished no hopes of bliss beyond the grave to compensate for the evils which he felt or imagined here. And if, in their bewildered conjectures as to the purpose of earthly existence, the banqueters should throw aside the veil, and cast an inquiring glance at this figure of death, as seeking thence the solution otherwise unattainable, the only reply would be a stare of the vacant eye-caverns and a grin of the skeleton jaws. Such was the response that the dead man had fancied himself to receive when he asked of Death to solve the riddle of his life; and it was his desire to repeat it when the guests of his dismal hospitality should find themselves perplexed with the same question.

"What means that wreath?" asked several of the company, while viewing the decorations of the table.

They alluded to a wreath of cypress, which was held on high by a skeleton arm, protruding from within the black mantle.

"It is a crown," said one of the stewards, "not for the worthiest, but for the wofulest, when he shall prove his claim to it."

The guest earliest bidden to the festival was a man of soft and gentle character, who had not energy to struggle against the heavy despondency to which his temperament rendered him liable; and therefore with nothing outwardly to excuse him from happiness, he had spent a life of quiet misery that made his blood torpid, and weighed upon his breath, and sat like a ponderous night-fiend upon every throb of his unresisting heart. His wretchedness seemed as deep as his original nature, if not identical with it. It was the misfortune of a second guest to cherish within his bosom a diseased heart, which had become so wretchedly sore that the continual and unavoidable rubs of the world, the blow of an enemy, the careless jostle of a stranger, and even the faithful and loving touch of a friend, alike made ulcers in it. As is the habit of people thus afflicted, he found his chief employment in exhibiting these miserable sores to any who would give themselves the pain of viewing them. A third guest was a hypochondriac, whose imagination wrought necromancy in his outward and inward world, and caused him to see monstrous faces in the household fire, and dragons in the clouds of sunset, and fiends in the guise of beautiful women, and something ugly or wicked beneath all the pleasant surfaces of nature. His neighbor at table was one who, in his early youth, had trusted mankind too much, and hoped too highly in their behalf, and, in meeting with many disappointments, had become desperately soured. For several years back this misanthrope bad employed himself in accumulating motives for hating and despising his race,—such as murder, lust, treachery, ingratitude, faithlessness of trusted friends, instinctive vices of children, impurity of women, hidden guilt in men of saint-like aspect,—and, in short, all manner of black realities that sought to decorate themselves with outward grace or glory. But at every atrocious fact that was added to his catalogue, at every increase of the sad knowledge which he spent his life to collect, the native impulses of the poor man's loving and confiding heart made him groan with anguish. Next, with his heavy brow bent downward, there stole into the hall a man naturally earnest and impassioned, who, from his immemorial infancy, had felt the consciousness of a high message to the world; but, essaying to deliver it, had found either no voice or form of speech, or else no ears to listen. Therefore his whole life was a bitter questioning of himself: "Why have not men acknowledged my mission? Am I not a self-deluding fool? What business have I on earth? Where is my grave?" Throughout the festival, he quaffed frequent draughts from the sepulchral urn of wine, hoping thus to quench the celestial fire that tortured his own breast and could not benefit his race.

Then there entered, having flung away a ticket for a ball, a gay gallant of yesterday, who had found four or five wrinkles in his brow, and more gray hairs than he could well number on his head. Endowed with sense and feeling, he had nevertheless spent his youth in folly, but had reached at last that dreary point in life where Folly quits us of her own accord, leaving us to make friends with Wisdom if we can. Thus, cold and desolate, he had come to seek Wisdom at the banquet, and wondered if the skeleton were she. To eke out the company, the stewards had invited a distressed poet from his home in the almshouse, and a melancholy idiot from the street-corner. The latter had just the glimmering of sense that was sufficient to make him conscious of a vacancy, which the poor fellow, all his life long, had mistily sought to fill up with intelligence, wandering up and down the streets, and groaning miserably because his attempts were ineffectual. The only lady in the hall was one who had fallen short of absolute and perfect beauty, merely by the trifling defect of a slight cast in her left eye. But this blemish, minute as it was, so shocked the pure ideal of her soul, rather than her vanity, that she passed her life in solitude, and veiled her countenance even from her own gaze. So the skeleton sat shrouded at one end of the table, and this poor lady at the other.

One other guest remains to be described. He was a young man of smooth brow, fair cheek, and fashionable mien. So far as his exterior developed him, he might much more suitably have found a place at some merry Christmas table, than have been numbered among the blighted, fate-stricken, fancy-tortured set of ill-starred banqueters. Murmurs arose among the guests as they noted, the glance of general scrutiny which the intruder threw over his companions. What had he to do among them? Why did not the skeleton of the dead founder of the feast unbend its rattling joints, arise, and motion the unwelcome stranger from the board?

"Shameful!" said the morbid man, while a new ulcer broke out in his heart. "He comes to mock us! we shall be the jest of his tavern friends I—he will make a farce of our miseries, and bring it out upon the stage!"

"O, never mind him!" said the hypochondriac, smiling sourly. "He shall feast from yonder tureen of viper-soup; and if there is a fricassee of scorpions on the table, pray let him have his share of it. For the dessert, he shall taste the apples of Sodom, then, if he like our Christmas fare, let him return again next year!"

"Trouble him not," murmured the melancholy man, with gentleness. "What matters it whether the consciousness of misery come a few years sooner or later? If this youth deem himself happy now, yet let him sit with us for the sake of the wretchedness to come."

The poor idiot approached the young man with that mournful aspect of vacant inquiry which his face continually wore, and which caused people to say that he was always in search of his missing wits. After no little examination he touched the stranger's hand, but immediately drew back his own, shaking his head and shivering.

"Cold, cold, cold!" muttered the idiot.

The young man shivered too, and smiled.

"Gentlemen, and you, madam," said one of the stewards of the festival, "do not conceive so ill either of our caution or judgment, as to imagine that we have admitted this young stranger—Gervayse Hastings by name—without a full investigation and thoughtful balance of his claims. Trust me, not a guest at the table is better entitled to his seat."

The steward's guaranty was perforce satisfactory. The company, therefore, took their places, and addressed themselves to the serious business of the feast, but were soon disturbed by the hypochondriac, who thrust back his chair, complaining that a dish of stewed toads and vipers was set before him, and that there was green ditchwater in his cup of wine. This mistake being amended, he quietly resumed his seat. The wine, as it flowed freely from the sepulchral urn, seemed to come imbued with all gloomy inspirations; so that its influence was not to cheer, but either to sink the revellers into a deeper melancholy, or elevate their spirits to an enthusiasm of wretchedness. The conversation was various. They told sad stories about people who might have been Worthy guests at such a festival as the present. They talked of grisly incidents in human history; of strange crimes, which, if truly considered, were but convulsions of agony; of some lives that had been altogether wretched, and of others, which, wearing a general semblance of happiness, had yet been deformed, sooner or later, by misfortune, as by the intrusion of a grim face at a banquet; of death-bed scenes, and what dark intimations might be gathered from the words of dying men; of suicide, and whether the more eligible mode were by halter, knife, poison, drowning, gradual starvation, or the fumes of charcoal. The majority of the guests, as is the custom with people thoroughly and profoundly sick at heart, were anxious to make their own woes the theme of discussion, and prove themselves most excellent in anguish. The misanthropist went deep into the philosophy of evil, and wandered about in the darkness, with now and then a gleam of discolored light hovering on ghastly shapes and horrid scenery. Many a miserable thought, such as men have stumbled upon from age to age, did he now rake up again, and gloat over it as an inestimable gem, a diamond, a treasure far preferable to those bright, spiritual revelations of a better world, which are like precious stones from heaven's pavement. And then, amid his lore of wretchedness he hid his face and wept.

It was a festival at which the woful man of Uz might suitably have been a guest, together with all, in each succeeding age, who have tasted deepest of the bitterness of life. And be it said, too, that every son or daughter of woman, however favored with happy fortune, might, at one sad moment or another, have claimed the privilege of a stricken heart, to sit down at this table. But, throughout the feast, it was remarked that the young stranger, Gervayse Hastings, was unsuccessful in his attempts to catch its pervading spirit. At any deep, strong thought that found utterance, and which was torn out, as it were, from the saddest recesses of human consciousness, he looked mystified and bewildered; even more than the poor idiot, who seemed to grasp at such things with his earnest heart, and thus occasionally to comprehend them. The young man's conversation was of a colder and lighter kind, often brilliant, but lacking the powerful characteristics of a nature that had been developed by suffering.

"Sir," said the misanthropist, bluntly, in reply to some

observation by Gervayse Hastings, "pray do not address me again. We have no right to talk together. Our minds have nothing in common. By what claim you appear at this banquet I cannot guess; but methinks, to a man who could say what you have just now said, my companions and myself must seem no more than shadows flickering on the wall. And precisely such a shadow are you to us."

The young man smiled and bowed, but, drawing himself back in his chair, he buttoned his coat over his breast, as if the banqueting-ball were growing chill. Again the idiot fixed his melancholy stare upon the youth, and murmured, "Cold! cold! cold!"

The banquet drew to its conclusion, and the guests departed. Scarcely had they stepped across the threshold of the hall, when the scene that had there passed seemed like the vision of a sick fancy, or an exhalation from a stagnant heart. Now and then, however, during the year that ensued, these melancholy people caught glimpses of one another, transient, indeed, but enough to prove that they walked the earth with the ordinary allotment of reality. Sometimes a pair of them came face to face, while stealing through the evening twilight, enveloped in their sable cloaks. Sometimes they casually met in churchyards. Once, also, it happened that two of the dismal banqueters mutually started at recognizing each other in the noonday sunshine of a crowded street, stalking there like ghosts astray. Doubtless they wondered why the skeleton did not come abroad at noonday too.

But whenever the necessity of their affairs compelled these Christmas guests into the bustling world, they were sure to encounter the young man who had so unaccountably been admitted to the festival. They saw him among the gay and fortunate; they caught the sunny sparkle of his eye; they heard the light and careless tones of his voice, and muttered to themselves with such indignation as only the aristocracy of wretchedness could kindle, "The traitor! The vile impostor!

Providence, in its own good time, may give him a right to feast among us!" But the young man's unabashed eye dwelt upon their gloomy figures as they passed him, seeming to say, perchance with somewhat of a sneer, "First, know my secret then, measure your claims with mine!"

The step of Time stole onward, and soon brought merry Christmas round again, with glad and solemn worship in the churches, and sports, games, festivals, and everywhere the bright face of Joy beside the household fire. Again likewise the hall, with its curtains of dusky purple, was illuminated by the death-torches gleaming on the sepulchral decorations of the banquet. The veiled, skeleton sat in state, lifting the cypress-wreath above its head, as the guerdon of some guest illustrious in the qualifications which there claimed precedence. As the stewards deemed the world inexhaustible in misery, and were desirous of recognizing it in all its forms, they had not seen fit to reassemble the company of the former year. New faces now threw their gloom across the table.

There was a man of nice conscience, who bore a blood-stain in his heart—the death of a fellow-creature—which, for his more exquisite torture, had chanced with such a peculiarity of circumstances, that he could not absolutely determine whether his will had entered into the deed or not. Therefore, his whole life was spent in the agony of an inward trial for murder, with a continual sifting of the details of his terrible calamity, until his mind had no longer any thought, nor his soul any emotion, disconnected with it, There was a mother, too,—a mother once, but a desolation now,—who, many years before, had gone out on a pleasure-party, and, returning, found her infant smothered in its little bed. And ever since she has been tortured with the fantasy that her buried baby lay smothering in its coffin. Then there was an aged lady, who had lived from time immemorial with a constant tremor quivering through her-frame. It was terrible to discern her dark shadow tremulous upon the wall;

her lips, likewise, were tremulous; and the expression of her eye seemed to indicate that her soul was trembling too. Owing to the bewilderment and confusion which made almost a chaos of her intellect, it was impossible to discover what dire misfortune had thus shaken her nature to its depths; so that the stewards had admitted her to the table, not from any acquaintance with her history, but on the safe testimony of her miserable aspect. Some surprise was expressed at the presence of a bluff, red-faced gentleman, a certain Mr. Smith, who had evidently the fat of many a rich feast within him, and the habitual twinkle of whose eye betrayed a disposition to break forth into uproarious laughter for little cause or none. It turned out, however, that, with the best possible flow of spirits, our poor friend was afflicted with a physical disease of the heart, which threatened instant death on the slightest cachinnatory indulgence, or even that titillation of the bodily frame produced by merry thoughts. In this dilemma he had sought admittance to the banquet, on the ostensible plea of his irksome and miserable state, but, in reality, with the hope of imbibing a life-preserving melancholy.

A married couple had been invited from a motive of bitter humor, it being well understood that they rendered each other unutterably miserable whenever they chanced to meet, and therefore must necessarily be fit associates at the festival. In contrast with these was another couple still unmarried, who had interchanged their hearts in early life, but had been divided by circumstances as impalpable as morning mist, and kept apart so long that their spirits now found it impossible to meet, Therefore, yearning for communion, yet shrinking from one another and choosing none beside, they felt themselves companionless in life, and looked upon eternity as a boundless desert. Next to the skeleton sat a mere son of earth,—a hunter of the Exchange,—a gatherer of shining dust,—a man whose life's record was in his ledger, and whose soul's prison-house the vaults of the bank where he kept his deposits. This person had been greatly perplexed at his invitation, deeming himself one of the most fortunate men in the city; but the stewards persisted in demanding his presence, assuring him that he had no conception how miserable he was.

And now appeared a figure which we must acknowledge as our acquaintance of the former festival. It was Gervayse Hastings, whose presence had then caused so much question and criticism, and who now took his place with the composure of one whose claims were satisfactory to himself and must needs be allowed by others. Yet his easy and unruffled face betrayed no sorrow.

The well-skilled beholders gazed a moment into his eyes and shook their heads, to miss the unuttered sympathy—the countersign never to be falsified—of those whose hearts are cavern-mouths through which they descend into a region of illimitable woe and recognize other wanderers there.

"Who is this youth?" asked the man with a bloodstain on his conscience. "Surely he has never gone down into the depths! I know all the aspects of those who have passed through the dark valley. By what right is he among us?"

"Ah, it is a sinful thing to come hither without a sorrow," murmured the aged lady, in accents that partook of the eternal tremor which pervaded her whole being "Depart, young man! Your soul has never been shaken, and, therefore, I tremble so much the more to look at you."

"His soul shaken! No; I'll answer for it," said bluff Mr. Smith, pressing his hand upon his heart and making himself as melancholy as he could, for fear of a fatal explosion of laughter. "I know the lad well; he has as fair prospects as any young man about town, and has no more right among us miserable creatures than the child unborn. He never was miserable and probably never will be!"

"Our honored guests," interposed the stewards, "pray have

patience with us, and believe, at least, that our deep veneration for the sacredness of this solemnity would preclude any wilful violation of it. Receive this young man to your table. It may not be too much to say, that no guest here would exchange his own heart for the one that beats within that youthful bosom!"

"I'd call it a bargain, and gladly, too," muttered Mr. Smith, with a perplexing mixture of sadness and mirthful conceit. "A plague upon their nonsense! My own heart is the only really miserable one in the company; it will certainly be the death of me at last!"

Nevertheless, as on the former occasion, the judgment of the stewards being without appeal, the company sat down. The obnoxious guest made no more attempt to obtrude his conversation on those about him, but appeared to listen to the table-talk with peculiar assiduity, as if some inestimable secret, otherwise beyond his reach, might be conveyed in a casual word. And in truth, to those who could understand and value it, there was rich matter in the upgushings and outpourings of these initiated souls to whom sorrow had been a talisman, admitting them into spiritual depths which no other spell can open. Sometimes out of the midst of densest gloom there flashed a momentary radiance, pure as crystal, bright as the flame of stars, and shedding such a glow upon the mysteries of life, that the guests were ready to exclaim, "Surely the riddle is on the point of being solved!" At such illuminated intervals the saddest mourners felt it to be revealed that mortal griefs are but shadowy and external; no more than the sable robes voluminously shrouding a certain divine reality, and thus indicating what might otherwise be altogether invisible to mortal eye.

"Just now," remarked the trembling old woman, "I seemed to see beyond the outside. And then my everlasting tremor passed away!"

"Would that I could dwell always in these momentary gleams

of light!" said the man of stricken conscience. "Then the blood-stain in my heart would be washed clean away."

This strain of conversation appeared so unintelligibly absurd to good Mr. Smith, that he burst into precisely the fit of laughter which his physicians had warned him against, as likely to prove instantaneously fatal. In effect, he fell back in his chair a corpse, with a broad grin upon his face, while his ghost, perchance, remained beside it bewildered at its unpremeditated exit. This catastrophe of course broke up the festival.

"How is this? You do not tremble!" observed the tremulous old woman to Gervayse Hastings, who was gazing at the dead man with singular intentness. "Is it not awful to see him so suddenly vanish out of the midst of life,—this man of flesh and blood, whose earthly nature was so warm and strong? There is a never-ending tremor in my soul, but it trembles afresh at, this! And you are calm!"

"Would that he could teach me somewhat!" said Gervayse Hastings, drawing a long breath. "Men pass before me like shadows on the wall; their actions, passions, feelings, are flickerings of the light, and then they vanish! Neither the corpse, nor yonder skeleton, nor this old woman's everlasting tremor, can give me what I seek."

And then the company departed.

We cannot linger to narrate, in such detail, more circumstances of these singular festivals, which, in accordance with the founder's will, continued to be kept with the regularity of an established institution. In process of time the stewards adopted the custom of inviting, from far and near, those individuals whose misfortunes were prominent above other men's, and whose mental and moral development might, therefore, be supposed to possess a corresponding interest. The exiled noble of the French Revolution, and the broken soldier of the Empire, were alike represented at the table. Fallen monarchs, wandering about the earth, have found places at that forlorn and miserable feast. The statesman, when his party flung him off, might, if he chose it, be once more a great man for the space of a single banquet. Aaron Burr's name appears on the record at a period when his ruin—the profoundest and most striking, with more of moral circumstance in it than that of almost any other man—was complete in his lonely age. Stephen Guard, when his wealth weighed upon him like a mountain, once sought admittance of his own accord. It is not probable, however, that these men had any lesson to teach in the lore of discontent and misery which might not equally well have been studied in the common walks of life. Illustrious unfortunates attract a wider sympathy, not because their griefs are more intense, but because, being set on lofty pedestals, they the better serve mankind as instances and bywords of calamity.

It concerns our present purpose to say that, at each successive festival, Gervayse Hastings showed his face, gradually changing from the smooth beauty of his youth to the thoughtful comeliness of manhood, and thence to the bald, impressive dignity of age. He was the only individual invariably present. Yet on every occasion there were murmurs, both from those who knew his character and position, and from them whose hearts shrank back as denying his companionship in their mystic fraternity.

"Who is this impassive man?" had been asked a hundred times. "Has he suffered? Has he sinned? There are no traces of either. Then wherefore is he here?"

"You must inquire of the stewards or of himself," was the constant reply. "We seem to know him well here in our city, and know nothing of him but what is creditable and fortunate. Yet hither he comes, year after year, to this gloomy banquet, and sits among the guests like a marble statue. Ask yonder skeleton, perhaps that may solve the riddle!"

It was in truth a wonder. The life of Gervayse Hastings was not merely a prosperous, but a brilliant one. Everything had gone well with him. He was wealthy, far beyond the expenditure that was required by habits of magnificence, a taste of rare purity and cultivation, a love of travel, a scholar's instinct to collect a splendid library, and, moreover, what seemed a magnificent liberality to the distressed. He had sought happiness, and not vainly, if a lovely and tender wife, and children of fair promise, could insure it. He had, besides, ascended above the limit which separates the obscure from the distinguished, and had won a stainless reputation in affairs of the widest public importance. Not that he was a popular character, or had within him the mysterious attributes which are essential to that species of success. To the public he was a cold abstraction, wholly destitute of those rich lines of personality, that living warmth, and the peculiar faculty of stamping his own heart's impression on a multitude of hearts, by which the people recognize their favorites. And it must be owned that, after his most intimate associates had done their best to know him thoroughly, and love him warmly, they were startled to find how little hold he had upon their affections. They approved, they admired, but still in those moments when the human spirit most craves reality, they shrank back from Gervayse Hastings, as powerless to give them what they sought. It was the feeling of distrustful regret with which we should draw back the hand after extending it, in an illusive twilight, to grasp the hand of a shadow upon the wall.

As the superficial fervency of youth decayed, this peculiar effect of Gervayse Hastings's character grew more perceptible. His children, when he extended his arms, came coldly to his knees, but never climbed them of their own accord. His wife wept secretly, and almost adjudged herself a criminal because she shivered in the chill of his bosom. He, too, occasionally appeared not unconscious of the chillness of his moral atmosphere, and willing, if it might be so, to warm himself at a kindly fire.

But age stole onward and benumbed him snore and more. As the hoar-frost began to gather on him his wife went to her grave, and was doubtless warmer there; his children either died or were scattered to different homes of their own; and old Gervayse Hastings, unscathed by grief,—alone, but needing no companionship,—continued his steady walk through life, and still one very Christmas day attended at the dismal banquet. His privilege as a guest had become prescriptive now. Had he claimed the head of the table, even the skeleton would have been ejected from its seat.

Finally, at the merry Christmas-tide, when he had numbered fourscore years complete, this pale, highbrowed, marble-featured old man once more entered the long-frequented hall, with the same impassive aspect that had called forth so much dissatisfied remark at his first attendance. Time, except in matters merely external, had done nothing for him, either of good or evil. As he took his place he threw a calm, inquiring glance around the table, as if to ascertain whether any guest had yet appeared, after so many unsuccessful banquets, who might impart to him the mystery—the deep, warm secret—the life within the life—which, whether manifested in joy or sorrow, is what gives substance to a world of shadows.

"My friends," said Gervayse Hastings, assuming a position which his long conversance with the festival caused to appear natural, "you are welcome! I drink to you all in this cup of sepulchral wine."

The guests replied courteously, but still in a manner that proved them unable to receive the old man as a member of their sad fraternity. It may be well to give the reader an idea of the present company at the banquet.

One was formerly a clergyman, enthusiastic in his profession, and apparently of the genuine dynasty of those old Puritan divines whose faith in their calling, and stern exercise of it, had placed them among the mighty of the earth. But yielding to the speculative tendency of the age, he had gone astray from the firm foundation of an ancient faith, and wandered into a cloud-region, where everything was misty and deceptive, ever mocking him with a semblance of reality, but still dissolving when he flung himself upon it for support and rest. His instinct and early training demanded something steadfast; but, looking forward, he beheld vapors piled on vapors, and behind him an impassable gulf between the man of yesterday and to-day, on the borders of which he paced to and fro, sometimes wringing his hands in agony, and often making his own woe a theme of scornful merriment. This surely was a miserable man. Next, there was a theorist,—one of a numerous tribe, although he deemed himself unique since the creation,—a theorist, who had conceived a plan by which all the wretchedness of earth, moral and physical, might be done away, and the bliss of the millennium at once accomplished. But, the incredulity of mankind debarring him from action, he was smitten with as much grief as if the whole mass of woe which he was denied the opportunity to remedy were crowded into his own bosom. A plain old man in black attracted much of the company's notice, on the supposition that he was no other than Father Miller, who, it seemed, had given himself up to despair at the tedious delay of the final conflagration. Then there was a man distinguished for native pride and obstinacy, who, a little while before, had possessed immense wealth, and held the control of a vast moneyed interest which he had wielded in the same spirit as a despotic monarch would wield the power of his empire, carrying on a tremendous moral warfare, the roar and tremor of which was felt at every fireside in the land. At length came a crushing ruin,—a total overthrow of fortune, power, and character,—the effect of which on his imperious and, in many respects, noble and lofty nature might have entitled him to a place, not merely at our festival, but among the peers of Pandemonium.

There was a modern philanthropist, who had become so deeply sensible of the calamities of thousands and millions of his fellow-creatures, and of the impracticableness of any general measures for their relief, that he had no heart to do what little good lay immediately within his power, but contented himself with being miserable for sympathy. Near him sat a gentleman in a predicament hitherto unprecedented, but of which the present epoch probably affords numerous examples. Ever since he was of capacity to read a newspaper, this person had prided himself on his consistent adherence to one political party, but, in the confusion of these latter days, had got bewildered and knew not whereabouts his party was. This wretched condition, so morally desolate and disheartening to a man who has long accustomed himself to merge his individuality in the mass of a great body, can only be conceived by such as have experienced it. His next companion was a popular orator who had lost his voice, and—as it was pretty much all that he had to lose—had fallen into a state of hopeless melancholy. The table was likewise graced by two of the gentler sex,—one, a half-starved, consumptive seamstress, the representative of thousands just as wretched; the other, a woman of unemployed energy, who found herself in the world with nothing to achieve, nothing to enjoy, and nothing even to suffer. She had, therefore, driven herself to the verge of madness by dark broodings over the wrongs of her sex, and its exclusion from a proper field of action. The roll of guests being thus complete, a side-table had been set for three or four disappointed office-seekers, with hearts as sick as death, whom the stewards had admitted partly because their calamities really entitled them to entrance here, and partly that they were in especial need of a good dinner. There was likewise a homeless dog, with his tail between his legs, licking up the crumbs and gnawing the fragments of the feast,—such a melancholy cur as one sometimes sees about the streets without a master, and willing to follow the first that will accept his service.

In their own way, these were as wretched a set of people as ever had assembled at the festival. There they sat, with the veiled skeleton of the founder holding aloft the cypress-wreath, at one end of the table, and at the other, wrapped in furs, the withered figure of Gervayse Hastings, stately, calm, and cold, impressing the company with awe, yet so little interesting their sympathy that he might have vanished into thin air without their once exclaiming, "Whither is he gone?"

"Sir," said the philanthropist, addressing the old man, "you have been so long a guest at this annual festival, and have thus been conversant with so many varieties of human affliction, that, not improbably, you have thence derived some great and important lessons. How blessed were your lot could you reveal a secret by which all this mass of woe might be removed!"

"I know of but one misfortune," answered Gervayse Hastings, quietly, "and that is my own."

"Your own!" rejoined the philanthropist. "And looking back on your serene and prosperous life, how can you claim to be the sole unfortunate of the human race?"

"You will not understand it," replied Gervayse Hastings, feebly, and with a singular inefficiency of pronunciation, and sometimes putting one word for another. "None have understood it, not even those who experience the like. It is a chillness, a want of earnestness, a feeling as if what should be my heart were a thing of vapor, a haunting perception of unreality! Thus seeming to possess all that other men have, all that men aim at, I have really possessed nothing, neither joy nor griefs. All things, all persons,—as was truly said to me at this table long and long ago,—have been like shadows flickering on the wall. It was so with my wife and children, with those who seemed my friends: it is so with yourselves, whom I see now before one. Neither have I myself any real existence, but am a shadow like the rest."

"And how is it with your views of a future life?" inquired the speculative clergyman.

"Worse than with you," said the old man, in a hollow and feeble tone; "for I cannot conceive it earnestly enough to feel either hope or fear. Mine,—mine is the wretchedness! This cold heart, —this unreal life! Ah! it grows colder still."

It so chanced that at this juncture the decayed ligaments of the skeleton gave way, and the dry hones fell together in a heap, thus causing the dusty wreath of cypress to drop upon the table. The attention of the company being thus diverted for a single instant from Gervayse Hastings, they perceived, on turning again towards him, that the old man had undergone a change. His shadow had ceased to flicker on the wall.

"Well, Rosina, what is your criticism?" asked Roderick, as he rolled up the manuscript.

"Frankly, your success is by no means complete," replied she. "It is true, I have an idea of the character you endeavor to describe; but it is rather by dint of my own thought than your expression."

"That is unavoidable," observed the sculptor, "because the characteristics are all negative. If Gervayse Hastings could have imbibed one human grief at the gloomy banquet, the task of describing him would have been infinitely easier. Of such persons—and we do meet with these moral monsters now and then—it is difficult to conceive how they came to exist here, or what there is in them capable of existence hereafter. They seem to be on the outside of everything; and nothing wearies the soul more than an attempt to comprehend them within its grasp."

MORTIMER'S ORPHANAGE

By Gabriel

This ultra short story, Mortimer's Orphanage from British author Gabriel is a dark one, it's best to take a deep breath before diving in if you are of a nervous disposition...

MORTIMER'S ORPHANAGE

As the clock ticked past one minute to midnight on Christmas eve, the gaunt bodies of the children at Mortimer's orphanage huddled together. Their bodies akin to skeletons dipped in latex, one would marvel at how they were still able to draw breath.

Their eyes watched the clock, drinking in each second until "he" would arrive. But not Father Christmas. This was something else.

Every Christmas "he" would arrive, "his" jolly form sweeping through the room, the children clamouring to be close to "his" touch, desperate to be chosen. Believing the creature would take lucky ones to be adopted, to a land of bedtime stories, warm beds and warmer hugs.

But alas, this was just a fallacy concocted by the owner of Mortimer's Orphanage, a heartless being who doesn't deserve to be considered human.

The truth was something much darker.

The children couldn't see beyond the glamour as every Christmas "it" arrived dressed in darkness, a formless being of shadows, sweeping through the room taking children at will. Each Christmas gifting Mortimer an extra year on Earth.

The clock struck midnight.

Something darker than night itself entered the room...

BETWEEN THE LIGHTS

By E.F. Benson

"Between the Lights" by Edward Frederic Benson is a classic English country house Christmas ghost story, first published in 1912 in a collection titled 'The Room in the Tower and Other Stories', which featured several of Benson's supernatural and ghostly tales. Set the day before Christmas, the narrative unfolds as a group of friends gathers during the twilight hours, sharing eerie tales in the dimming light. Everard Chandler, the narrator, recounts an unsettling experience where he witnesses a mysterious and shadowy figure on the croquet lawn...

BETWEEN THE LIGHTS

The day had been one unceasing fall of snow from sunrise until the gradual withdrawal of the vague white light outside indicated that the sun had set again. But as usual at this hospitable and delightful house of Everard Chandler where I often spent Christmas, and was spending it now, there had been no lack of entertainment, and the hours had passed with a rapidity that had surprised us. A short billiard tournament had filled up the time between breakfast and lunch, with Badminton and the morning papers for those who were temporarily not engaged, while afterwards, the interval till tea-time had been occupied by the majority of the party in a huge game of hide-and-seek all over the house, barring the billiard-room, which was sanctuary for any who desired peace. But few had done that; the enchantment of Christmas, I must suppose, had, like some spell, made children of us again, and it was with palsied terror and trembling misgivings that we had tip-toed up and down the dim passages, from any corner of which some wild screaming form might dart out on us. Then, wearied with exercise and emotion, we had assembled again for tea in the hall, a room of shadows and panels on which the light from the wide open fireplace, where there burned a divine mixture of peat and logs, flickered and grew bright again on the walls. Then, as was proper, ghost-stories, for the narration of which the electric light was put out, so that the listeners might conjecture anything they pleased to be lurking in the corners, succeeded, and we vied with each other in blood, bones, skeletons, armour and shrieks. I had, just given my contribution, and was reflecting with some complacency that probably the worst was now known, when Everard, who had not yet administered to the horror of his guests, spoke. He was sitting opposite me in the full blaze of the fire, looking, after the illness he had gone through during the autumn, still rather pale and delicate. All the same he had been among the boldest and best in the exploration of dark places that afternoon, and the look on his face now rather startled me.

"No, I don't mind that sort of thing," he said. "The paraphernalia of ghosts has become somehow rather hackneyed, and when I hear of screams and skeletons I feel I am on familiar ground, and can at least hide my head under the bed-clothes."

"Ah, but the bed-clothes were twitched away by my skeleton," said I, in self-defence.

"I know, but I don't even mind that. Why, there are seven, eight skeletons in this room now, covered with blood and skin and other horrors. No, the nightmares of one's childhood were the really frightening things, because they were vague. There was the true atmosphere of horror about them because one didn't know what one feared. Now if one could recapture that–"

Mrs. Chandler got quickly out of her seat.

"Oh, Everard," she said, "surely you don't wish to recapture it again. I should have thought once was enough."

This was enchanting. A chorus of invitation asked him to proceed: the real true ghost-story first-hand, which was what seemed to be indicated, was too precious a thing to lose.

Everard laughed. "No, dear, I don't want to recapture it again at all," he said to his wife.

Then to us: "But really the–well, the nightmare perhaps, to which I was referring, is of the vaguest and most unsatisfactory kind. It has no apparatus about it at all. You will probably all say that it was nothing, and wonder why I was frightened. But I was; it frightened me out of my wits. And I only just saw something, without being able to swear what it was, and heard something which might have been a falling stone."

"Anyhow, tell us about the falling stone," said I.

There was a stir of movement about the circle round the fire, and the movement was not of purely physical order. It was as if–this is only what I personally felt–it was as if the childish gaiety of the hours we had passed that day was suddenly withdrawn; we had jested on certain subjects, we had played hide-and-seek with all the power of earnestness that was in us. But now–so it seemed to me–there was going to be real hide-and-seek, real terrors were going to lurk in dark corners, or if not real terrors, terrors so convincing as to assume the garb of reality, were going to pounce on us. And Mrs. Chandler's exclamation as she sat down again, "Oh, Everard, won't it excite you?" tended in any case to excite us. The room still remained in dubious darkness except for the sudden lights disclosed on the walls by the leaping flames on the hearth, and there was wide field for conjecture as to what might lurk in the dim corners. Everard, moreover, who had been sitting in bright light before, was banished by the extinction of some flaming log into the shadows. A voice alone spoke to us, as he sat back in his low chair, a voice rather slow but very distinct.

"Last year," he said, "on the twenty-fourth of December, we were down here, as usual, Amy and I, for Christmas. Several of you who are here now were here then. Three or four of you at least."

I was one of these, but like the others kept silence, for the identification, so it seemed to me, was not asked for. And he went on again without a pause.

"Those of you who were here then," he said, "and are here now, will remember how very warm it was this day year. You will remember, too, that we played croquet that day on the lawn. It was perhaps a little cold for croquet, and we played it rather in order to be able to say–with sound evidence to back the statement–that we had done so."

Then he turned and addressed the whole little circle.

"We played ties of half-games," he said, "just as we have played billiards to-day, and it was certainly as warm on the lawn then as it was in the billiard-room this morning directly after breakfast, while to-day I should not wonder if there was three feet of snow outside. More, probably; listen."

A sudden draught fluted in the chimney, and the fire flared up as the current of air caught it.

The wind also drove the snow against the windows, and as he said, "Listen," we heard a soft scurry of the falling flakes against the panes, like the soft tread of many little people who stepped lightly, but with the persistence of multitudes who were flocking to some rendezvous. Hundreds of little feet seemed to be gathering outside; only the glass kept them out. And of the eight skeletons present four or five, anyhow, turned and looked at the windows. These were small-paned, with leaden bars. On the leaden bars little heaps of snow had accumulated, but there was nothing else to be seen.

"Yes, last Christmas Eve was very warm and sunny," went on Everard. "We had had no frost that autumn, and a temerarious dahlia was still in flower. I have always thought that it must have been mad."

He paused a moment.

"And I wonder if I were not mad too," he added.

No one interrupted him; there was something arresting, I must suppose, in what he was saying; it chimed in anyhow with the hide-and-seek, with the suggestions of the lonely snow.

Mrs. Chandler had sat down again, but I heard her stir in her chair. But never was there a gay party so reduced as we had been in the last five minutes. Instead of laughing at ourselves for playing silly games, we were all taking a serious game seriously.

"Anyhow, I was sitting out," he said to me, "while you and my wife played your half-game of croquet. Then it struck me that it was not so warm as I had supposed, because quite suddenly I shivered. And shivering I looked up. But I did not see you and her playing croquet at all. I saw something which had no relation to you and her–at least I hope not."

Now the angler lands his fish, the stalker kills his stag, and the speaker holds his audience.

And as the fish is gaffed, and as the stag is shot, so were we held. There was no getting away till he had finished with us.

"You all know the croquet lawn," he said, "and how it is bounded all round by a flower border with a brick wall behind it, through which, you will remember, there is only one gate.

"Well, I looked up and saw that the lawn–I could for one moment see it was still a lawn–was shrinking, and the walls closing in upon it. As they closed in too, they grew higher, and simultaneously the light began to fade and be sucked from the sky, till it grew quite dark overhead and only a glimmer of light came in through the gate.

"There was, as I told you, a dahlia in flower that day, and as this dreadful darkness and bewilderment came over me, I remember that my eyes sought it in a kind of despair, holding on, as it were, to any familiar object. But it was no longer a dahlia, and for the red of its petals I saw only the red of some feeble firelight. And at that moment the hallucination was complete. I was no longer sitting on the lawn watching croquet, but I was in a low-roofed room, something like a cattle-shed, but round. Close above my head, though I was sitting down, ran rafters from wall to wall. It was nearly dark, but a little light came in from the door opposite to me, which seemed to lead into a passage that communicated with the exterior of the place. Little, however, of the wholesome air came into this dreadful den; the atmosphere was oppressive and foul beyond all telling, it was as if for years it had been the place of some human menagerie, and for those years had been uncleaned and unsweetened by the winds of heaven. Yet that oppressiveness was nothing to the awful horror of the place from the view of the spirit. Some dreadful atmosphere of crime and abomination dwelt heavy in it, its denizens, whoever they were, were scarce human, so it seemed to me, and though men and women, were akin more to the beasts of the field. And in addition there was present to me some sense of the weight of years; I had been taken and thrust down into some epoch of dim antiquity."

He paused a moment, and the fire on the hearth leaped up for a second and then died down again. But in that gleam I saw that all faces were turned to Everard, and that all wore some look of dreadful expectancy. Certainly I felt it myself, and waited in a sort of shrinking horror for what was coming.

"As I told you," he continued, "where there had been that unseasonable dahlia, there now burned a dim firelight, and my eyes were drawn there. Shapes were gathered round it; what they were I could not at first see. Then perhaps my eyes got more accustomed to the dusk, or the fire burned better, for I perceived that they were of human form, but very small, for when one rose with a horrible chattering, to his feet, his head was still some inches off the low roof. He was dressed in a sort of shirt that came to his knees, but his arms were bare and covered with hair.

"Then the gesticulation and chattering increased, and I knew that they were talking about me, for they kept pointing in my direction. At that my horror suddenly deepened, for I became aware that I was powerless and could not move hand or foot; a helpless, nightmare impotence had possession of me. I could not lift a finger or turn my head. And in the paralysis of that fear I tried to scream, but not a sound could I utter.

"All this I suppose took place with the instantaneousness of a dream, for at once, and without transition, the whole thing had vanished, and I was back on the lawn again, while the stroke for which my wife was aiming was still unplayed. But my face was dripping with perspiration, and I was trembling all over.

"Now you may all say that I had fallen asleep, and had a sudden nightmare. That may be so; but I was conscious of no sense of sleepiness before, and I was conscious of none afterwards. It was as if someone had held a book before me, whisked the pages open for a second and closed them again."

Somebody, I don't know who, got up from his chair with a sudden movement that made me start, and turned on the electric light. I do not mind confessing that I was rather glad of this.

Everard laughed.

"Really I feel like Hamlet in the play-scene," he said, "and as if there was a guilty uncle present. Shall I go on?"

I don't think anyone replied, and he went on.

"Well, let us say for the moment that it was not a dream exactly, but a hallucination.

"Whichever it was, in any case it haunted me; for months, I think, it was never quite out of my mind, but lingered somewhere in the dusk of consciousness, sometimes sleeping quietly, so to speak, but sometimes stirring in its sleep. It was no good my telling myself that I was disquieting myself in vain, for it was as if something had actually entered into my very soul, as if some seed of horror had been planted there. And as the weeks went on the seed began to sprout, so that I could no longer even tell myself that that vision had been a moment's disorderment only. I can't say that it actually affected my health. I did not, as far as I know, sleep or eat insufficiently, but morning after morning I used to wake, not gradually and through pleasant dozings into full consciousness, but with absolute suddenness, and find myself plunged in an abyss of despair.

"Often too, eating or drinking, I used to pause and wonder if it was worth while.

"Eventually, I told two people about my trouble, hoping that perhaps the mere communication would help matters, hoping also, but very distantly, that though I could not believe at present that digestion or the obscurities of the nervous system were at fault, a doctor by some simple dose might convince me of it. In other words I told my wife, who laughed at me, and my doctor, who laughed also, and assured me that my health was quite unnecessarily robust.

"At the same time he suggested that change of air and scene does wonders for the delusions that exist merely in the imagination. He also told me, in answer to a direct question, that he would stake his reputation on the certainty that I was not going mad.

"Well, we went up to London as usual for the season, and though nothing whatever occurred to remind me in any way of that single moment on Christmas Eve, the reminding was seen to all right, the moment itself took care of that, for instead of fading as is the way of sleeping or waking dreams, it grew every day more vivid, and ate, so to speak, like some corrosive acid into my mind, etching itself there. And to London succeeded Scotland.

"I took last year for the first time a small forest up in Sutherland, called Glen Callan, very remote and wild, but affording excellent stalking. It was not far from the sea, and the gillies used always to warn me to carry a compass on the hill, because sea-mists were liable to come up with frightful rapidity, and there was always a danger of being caught by one, and of having perhaps to wait hours till it cleared again. This at first I always used to do, but, as everyone knows, any precaution that one takes which continues to be unjustified gets gradually relaxed, and at the end of a few weeks, since the weather had been uniformly clear, it was natural that, as often as not, my compass remained at home.

"One day the stalk took me on to a part of my ground that I had seldom been on before, a very high table-land on the limit of my forest, which went down very steeply on one side to a loch that lay below it, and on the other, by gentler gradations, to the river that came from the loch, six miles below which stood the lodge. The wind had necessitated our climbing up–or so my stalker had insisted–not by the easier way, but up the crags from the loch. I had argued the point with him for it seemed to me that it was impossible that the deer could get our scent if we went by the more natural path, but he still held to his opinion; and therefore, since after all this was his part of the job, I yielded. A dreadful climb we had of it, over big boulders with deep holes in between, masked by clumps of heather, so that a wary eye and a prodding stick were necessary for each step if one wished to avoid broken bones. Adders also literally swarmed in the heather; we must have seen a dozen at least on our way up, and adders are a beast for which I have no manner of use. But a couple of hours saw us to the top, only to find that the stalker had been utterly at fault, and that the deer must quite infallibly have got wind of us, if they had remained in the place where we last saw them. That, when we could spy the ground again, we saw had happened; in any case they had gone. The man insisted the wind had changed, a palpably stupid excuse, and I wondered at that moment what other reason he had–for reason I felt sure there must be–for not wishing to take what would clearly now have been a better route. But this piece of bad management did not spoil our luck, for within an hour we had spied more deer, and about two o'clock I got a shot, killing a heavy stag. Then sitting on the heather I ate lunch, and enjoyed a well-earned bask and smoke in the sun. The pony meantime had been saddled with the stag, and was plodding homewards.

"The morning had been extraordinarily warm, with a little wind blowing off the sea, which lay a few miles off sparkling beneath a blue haze, and all morning in spite of our abominable climb I had had an extreme sense of peace, so much so that several times I had probed my mind, so to speak, to find if the horror still lingered there. But I could scarcely get any response from it.

"Never since Christmas had I been so free of fear, and it was with a great sense of repose, both physical and spiritual, that I lay looking up into the blue sky, watching my smoke-whorls curl slowly away into nothingness. But I was not allowed to take my ease long, for Sandy came and begged that I would move. The weather had changed, he said, the wind had shifted again, and he wanted me to be off this high ground and on the path again as soon as possible, because it looked to him as if a sea-mist would presently come up."

"'And yon's a bad place to get down in the mist,' he added, nodding towards the crags we had come up.

"I looked at the man in amazement, for to our right lay a gentle slope down on to the river, and there was now no possible reason for again tackling those hideous rocks up which we had climbed this morning. More than ever I was sure he had some secret reason for not wishing to go the obvious way. But about one thing he was certainly right, the mist was coming up from the sea, and I felt in my pocket for the compass, and found I had forgotten to bring it.

"Then there followed a curious scene which lost us time that we could really ill afford to waste, I insisting on going down by the way that common sense directed, he imploring me to take his word for it that the crags were the better way. Eventually, I marched off to the easier descent, and told him not to argue any more but follow. What annoyed me about him was that he would only give the most senseless reasons for preferring the crags. There were mossy places, he said, on the way I wished to go, a thing patently false, since the summer had been one spell of unbroken weather; or it was longer, also obviously untrue; or there were so many vipers about.

"But seeing that none of these arguments produced any effect, at last he desisted, and came after me in silence.

"We were not yet half down when the mist was upon us, shooting up from the valley like the broken water of a wave, and in three minutes we were enveloped in a cloud of fog so thick that we could barely see a dozen yards in front of us. It was therefore another cause for self-congratulation that we were not now, as we should otherwise have been, precariously clambering on the face of those crags up which we had come with such difficulty in the morning, and as I rather prided myself on my powers of generalship in the matter of direction, I continued leading, feeling sure that before long we should strike the track by the river. More than all, the absolute freedom from fear elated me; since Christmas I had not known the instinctive joy of that; I felt like a schoolboy home for the holidays. But the mist grew thicker and thicker, and whether it was that real rain-clouds had formed above it, or that it was of an extraordinary density itself, I got wetter in the next hour than I have ever been before or since. The wet seemed to penetrate the skin, and chill the very bones. And still there was no sign of the track for which I was making.

"Behind me, muttering to himself, followed the stalker, but his arguments and protestations were dumb, and it seemed as if he kept close to me, as if afraid.

"Now there are many unpleasant companions in this world; I would not, for instance, care to be on the hill with a drunkard or a maniac, but worse than either, I think, is a frightened man, because his trouble is infectious, and, insensibly. I began to be afraid of being frightened too.

"From that it is but a short step to fear. Other perplexities too beset us. At one time we seemed to be walking on flat ground, at another I felt sure we were climbing again, whereas all the time we ought to have been descending, unless we had missed the way very badly indeed. Also, for the month was October, it was beginning to get dark, and it was with a sense of relief that I remembered that the full moon would rise soon after sunset. But it had grown very much colder, and soon, instead of rain, we found we were walking through a steady fall of snow.

"Things were pretty bad, but then for the moment they seemed to mend, for, far away to the left, I suddenly heard the brawling of the river. It should, it is true, have been straight in front of me and we were perhaps a mile out of our way, but this was better than the blind wandering of the last hour, and turning to the left, I walked towards it. But before I had gone a hundred yards, I heard a sudden choked cry behind me, and just saw Sandy's form flying as if in terror of pursuit, into the mists. I called to him, but got no reply, and heard only the spurned stones of his running.

"What had frightened him I had no idea, but certainly with his disappearance, the infection of his fear disappeared also, and I went on, I may almost say, with gaiety. On the moment, however, I saw a sudden well-defined blackness in front of me, and before I knew what I was doing I was half stumbling, half walking up a very steep grass slope.

"During the last few minutes the wind had got up, and the driving snow was peculiarly uncomfortable, but there had been a certain consolation in thinking that the wind would soon disperse these mists, and I had nothing more than a moonlight walk home. But as I paused on this slope, I became aware of two things, one, that the blackness in front of me was very close, the other that, whatever it was, it sheltered me from the snow. So I climbed on a dozen yards into its friendly shelter, for it seemed to me to be friendly.

"A wall some twelve feet high crowned the slope, and exactly where I struck it there was a hole in it, or door rather, through which a little light appeared. Wondering at this I pushed on, bending down, for the passage was very low, and in a dozen yards came out on the other side.

"Just as I did this the sky suddenly grew lighter, the wind, I suppose, having dispersed the mists, and the moon, though not yet visible through the flying skirts of cloud, made sufficient illumination.

"I was in a circular enclosure, and above me there projected from the walls some four feet from the ground, broken stones which must have been intended to support a floor. Then simultaneously two things occurred.

"The whole of my nine months' terror came back to me, for I saw that the vision in the garden was fulfilled, and at the same moment I saw stealing towards me a little figure as of a man, but only about three foot six in height. That my eyes told me; my ears told me that he stumbled on a stone; my nostrils told me that the air I breathed was of an overpowering foulness, and my soul told me that it was sick unto death. I think I tried to scream, but could not; I know I tried to move and could not. And it crept closer.

"Then I suppose the terror which held me spellbound so spurred me that I must move, for next moment I heard a cry break from my lips, and was stumbling through the passage. I made one leap of it down the grass slope, and ran as I hope never to have to run again. What direction I took I did not pause to consider, so long as I put distance between me and that place. Luck, however, favoured me, and before long I struck the track by the river, and an hour afterwards reached the lodge.

"Next day I developed a chill, and as you know pneumonia laid me on my back for six weeks.

"Well, that is my story, and there are many explanations. You may say that I fell asleep on the lawn, and was reminded of that by finding myself, under discouraging circumstances, in an old Picts' castle, where a sheep or a goat that, like myself, had taken shelter from the storm, was moving about. Yes, there are hundreds of ways in which you may explain it. But the coincidence was an odd one, and those who believe in second sight might find an instance of their hobby in it."

"And that is all?" I asked.

"Yes, it was nearly too much for me. I think the dressing-bell has sounded."

AGNES HAWTHORNE

By Caitlin Vaughan

Next up, a palette cleanser from Scottish author Caitlin Vaughan with a refreshing tale of ghost stories and redemption. It must be Christmas time!

AGNES HAWTHORNE

I

It was hard to imagine that the small, snow-covered town of Kirkcaldy with its streets adorned with twinkling Christmas lights, and the air filled with the comforting scent of wood-burning stoves would harbor a chilling secret beneath its picturesque façade. It seemed more like a place where dreams of a white Christmas came true every year.

In any other setting Holly Cottage, would seem an elegant Victorian-era house, but the stories whispered through the generations of the cottages dark history seemed to infect the very fabric of the building until its eerie presence loomed on the edge of town.

Sarah, newly widowed and new to the area was unaware of the town's spectral legend or the dread that whispered through its quaint streets. She saw the stately inviting structure, adorned with intricate gingerbread trim and ivy-covered walls, she saw the haunting beauty of the house and how with a bit of a tidy up its windows could glint with the promise. She saw a chance to start again.

"We're home now, Isla," Sarah said to her daughter, her breath forming a cloud in the cold air. "This is our fresh start."

Isla, her small hand clutched in her mother's, peered at the house with wide, curious eyes. "It's so big, Mummy. Do you think there are ghosts?"

Sarah smiled and ruffled Isla's hair. "Oh, sweetie, there's no such thing as ghosts. Just stories to make old houses seem more exciting." It wouldn't take long for Sarah to find Holly Cottage had stories of it's own.

The rumours of Holly Cottage were numerous. They spoke of Agnes Hawthorne, a spectre condemned to wander the mansion's shadowy halls. A fire, a family tragedy, and a girl who would become Kirkcaldy's most enduring legend.

"She died on Christmas Eve," Mrs. Thompson, their neighbour, recounted, her voice hushed. "They say she was found lifeless in her room, but there was no explanation. Some believe it was the work of a malevolent spirit."

Sarah refused to find these stories unnerving and dismissed them as old wives' tales. She wouldn't let ghost stories and superstitions deter her from building a happy life for Isla in their new home.
Unbeknownst to Sarah, Isla had already begun to form a connection with Holly Cottage. When left alone, she'd sit in the reading nook by the bay window, whispering to someone invisible. Her laughter would ring through the house.

"Mummy, I have a friend!" Isla declared with an eerie innocence as she played with her toys one morning.

Sarah looked at her daughter with a warm smile. "That's wonderful, sweetie. What's your friend's name?"

Isla pointed to the empty space beside her on the bed. "Her name is Agnes. She's very nice, and she tells me stories." The blood drained from Sarah's face, and she shivered. She wanted to believe that Isla simply overheard the name in a snatch of conversation, but she felt an inexplicable chill crawl up her spine.

Sarah watched with growing unease as she realised that what she once took for Isla chattering away to herself were conversations with an unseen companion. Isla's play, once filled with the sounds of childhood joy, now seemingly echoed with haunting laughter.

The presence of Agnes Hawthorne, the ghost of Holly Cottage, began to make itself known.

II

As Christmas drew near, Sarah decided to host a Christmas party for the town. She was certain that she had started projecting the stories onto the house after hearing the stories from the townsfolk and she was certain that by inviting the townspeople into their home, she could dispel the rumours of Holly Cottage being haunted. Sarah believed in the power of human connection, of togetherness during the holidays, once the townsfolk saw a happy home she could to drive away their supernatural fears.

The party was a delightful gathering of laughter, warmth, and holiday cheer. The Christmas tree illuminated, the air fragrant with freshly baked cookies, and laughter filling the rooms. Sarah's determination to chase away the apparitions that plagued Holly Cottage was infectious, and guests soon let their guards down. People clinked glasses and the house filled with life.

However, as the evening wore on, strange occurrences began to intrude on the merriment. Glasses clinked on the tables, their crystal chimes startling the guests. Shadows seemingly twisted and writhed on the walls, like spectral dancers in the dim candlelight.

Whispers spread among the guests, each trying hold onto the previous joy of the evening by downplaying the disturbances as mere quirks of an old house. But the energy of the room had shifted from joy to unease.

Mrs. Thompson leaned in close to Sarah and muttered, "Sarah, I heard footsteps in the hallway. Is that your daughter?"

Sarah, her smile strained, replied, "I'm sure it's just Isla playing with her new friend."

Isla's voice cut through the room like an otherworldly echo, distinct and fearless. "Mummy, Agnes says she wants to play a game with everyone!"

A shiver rippled through the guests, and a silence as icy as the December air fell upon them. They knew that the party had taken a haunting turn.

The events of the party marked a turning point for Sarah. She could no longer ignore the inexplicable occurrences and the presence of Agnes Hawthorne. It was time to confront the ghostly figure and uncover the truth.

She lit a single candle in the living room and sat in a weathered armchair, gazing into the eerie darkness that clung to the corners of the room.

"Agnes," she whispered, her voice trembling. "I know you're here. If you can hear me, give me a sign."

The room grew colder, and the candle's flame flickered erratically. It was as if the very walls were trying to speak. A presence formed before her, a shadowy figure with hollow eyes, and Agnes's mournful voice began to speak.

"Agnes, we're not your enemies," Sarah continued. "I need to understand why you're still here. What's keeping you in this house?"

"I died on Christmas Eve," Agnes murmured, her words a chilling whisper. "They believed I was the one who set the fire that killed my parents, but I was innocent, Sarah. I am not the malevolent spirit they think I am."

Sarah, her eyes locked onto Agnes's spectral form, felt a pang of empathy. She couldn't ignore the desperation in the ghostly figure's voice. Agnes's story unfolded like a haunting melody of injustice and betrayal. She was falsely accused, her pleas falling on deaf ears.

"Agnes, I'm so sorry," Sarah said, tears in her eyes. "I'll help you, I promise. We'll find a way to clear your name, to give you the peace you deserve."

III

Enlisting the help of her neighbour Sarah and Mrs. Thompson descended into the town archives, digging through the dusty remnants of the past.

"Look at this, Mrs. Thompson." Sarah exclaimed, her voice filled with excitement, "It's a letter from Agnes's mother, written a month before her death. She talks about problems with the fireplace and her struggle to find a chimney sweep."

Mrs. Thompson leaned in, her eyes scanning the letter. "That would have been dangerous, it could easily have caused the fire."

Sarah's heart raced as the truth began to unravel before her. "The town had accused Agnes of starting the fire that killed her parents, but it was a tragic accident. She was innocent all along."

Mrs. Thompson nodded, her eyes filling with emotion. "We've spent so long vilifying her memory, believing her to be a malevolent spirit, the accusation against her was unjust, it's time to set the record straight."

As news spread through the town of the new evidence that had come to light, the presence of Agnes in Holly Cottage seemed to grow weaker. It was as though the truth was slowly freeing her from her spectral chains, and the dark shadows of the house felt lighter, as though a burden had been lifted.

The community, fuelled by the discovery, was determined to honour Agnes's memory and right the wrong of the past. They were not only unravelling the dark history of Holly Cottage but also providing closure for a tormented spirit.

On Christmas Eve, Sarah, Isla, and the townspeople gathered in the room where Agnes had been found lifeless over a century ago. They placed a single white lily on a makeshift altar, its pristine petals symbolizing innocence. As they lit candles and incense, a solemn hush descended upon the room.

With a collective voice, they paid tribute to Agnes, correcting the memory of the misunderstood woman who had lingered in the shadows for so long. The air seemed to ripple with emotions, and a gentle breeze filled the room, as if Agnes's spirit was finally finding peace.

The story of Holly Cottage had taken a new turn, as its reputation transformed from one of malevolence to one of redemption and justice. As the townspeople departed, Sarah and Isla remained behind, gazing at the Christmas tree with a sense of closure.

"This is our home, Isla," Sarah said softly, her voice filled with both sorrow and hope. "And now, it's a place of peace."

The snow fell gently outside, blanketing the town in a serene, white embrace. Mother and daughter sat together, knowing that they had helped Agnes find the peace she had longed for. It was a Christmas Eve they would never forget, he whispers of Agnes were finally at rest.

THE ASH-TREE

By M.R. James

"The Ash-Tree" by M.R. James is a wintry ghost story set in the late 17th and mid-18th centuries, first published in 1904 within the anthology 'Ghost Stories of an Antiquary'. The narrative revolves around Sir Matthew Fell, a powerful landowner involved in the conviction of Mrs. Mothersole as a witch in 1690. Shortly after her trial, Sir Matthew meets a mysterious and gruesome fate. Fifty years later, his grandson, Sir Richard, inherits the estate, encountering troubles linked to an ash tree within the property's grounds...

THE ASH-TREE

Everyone who has travelled over Eastern England knows the smaller country-houses with which it is studded – the rather dank little buildings, usually in the Italian style, surrounded with parks of some eighty to a hundred acres. For me they have always had a very strong attraction: with the grey paling of split oak, the noble trees, the meres with their reed-beds, and the line of distant woods. Then, I like the pillared portico – perhaps stuck on to a red-brick Queen Anne house which has been faced with stucco to bring it into line with the 'Grecian' taste of the end of the eighteenth century; the hall inside, going up to the roof, which hall ought always to be provided with a gallery and a small organ. I like the library, too, where you may find anything from a Psalter of the thirteenth century to a Shakespeare quarto. I like the pictures, of course; and perhaps most of all I like fancying what life in such a house was when it was first built, and in the piping times of landlords' prosperity, and not least now, when, if money is not so plentiful, taste is more varied and life quite as interesting. I wish to have one of these houses, and enough money to keep it together and entertain my friends in it modestly.

But this is a digression. I have to tell you of a curious series of events which happened in such a house as I have tried to describe. It is Castringham Hall in Suffolk. I think a good deal has been done to the building since the period of my story, but the essential features I have sketched are still there – Italian portico, square block of white house, older inside than out, park with fringe of woods, and mere. The one feature that marked out the house from a score of others is gone. As you looked at it from the park, you saw on the right a great old ash-tree growing within half a dozen yards of the wall, and almost or quite touching the building with its branches. I suppose it had stood there ever since Castringham ceased to be a fortified place, and since the moat was filled in and the Elizabethan dwelling-house built. At any rate, it had wellnigh attained its full dimensions in the year 1690.

In that year the district in which the Hall is situated was the scene of a number of witch-trials. It will be long, I think, before we arrive at a just estimate of the amount of solid reason – if there was any – which lay at the root of the universal fear of witches in old times. Whether the persons accused of this offence really did imagine that they were possessed of unusual powers of any kind; or whether they had the will at least, if not the power, of doing mischief to their neighbours; or whether all the confessions, of which there are so many, were extorted by the mere cruelty of the witch-finders – these are questions which are not, I fancy, yet solved. And the present narrative gives me pause. I cannot altogether sweep it away as mere invention. The reader must judge for himself.

Castringham contributed a victim to the auto-da-fé. Mrs Mothersole was her name, and she differed from the ordinary run of village witches only in being rather better off and in a more influential position. Efforts were made to save her by several reputable farmers of the parish. They did their best to testify to her character, and showed considerable anxiety as to the verdict of the jury.

But what seems to have been fatal to the woman was the evidence of the then proprietor of Castringham Hall – Sir Matthew Fell. He deposed to having watched her on three different occasions from his window, at the full of the moon, gathering sprigs 'from the ash-tree near my house'. She had climbed into the branches, clad only in her shift, and was cutting off small twigs with a peculiarly curved knife, and as she did so she seemed to be talking to herself. On each occasion Sir

Matthew had done his best to capture the woman, but she had always taken alarm at some accidental noise he had made, and all he could see when he got down to the garden was a hare running across the park in the direction of the village.

On the third night he had been at the pains to follow at his best speed, and had gone straight to Mrs Mothersole's house; but he had had to wait a quarter of an hour battering at her door, and then she had come out very cross, and apparently very sleepy, as if just out of bed; and he had no good explanation to offer of his visit.

Mainly on this evidence, though there was much more of a less striking and unusual kind from other parishioners, Mrs Mothersole was found guilty and condemned to die. She was hanged a week after the trial, with five or six more unhappy creatures, at Bury St Edmunds. Sir Matthew Fell, then Deputy-Sheriff, was present at the execution. It was a damp, drizzly March morning when the cart made its way up the rough grass hill outside Northgate, where the gallows stood. The other victims were apathetic or broken down with misery; but Mrs Mothersole was, as in life so in death, of a very different temper. Her 'poysonous Rage', as a reporter of the time puts it, 'did so work upon the Bystanders – yea, even upon the Hangman – that it was constantly affirmed of all that saw her that she presented the living Aspect of a mad Divell. Yet she offer'd no Resistance to the Officers of the Law; onely she looked upon those that laid Hands upon her with so direful and venomous an Aspect that – as one of them afterwards assured me – the meer Thought of it preyed inwardly upon his Mind for six Months after.'

However, all that she is reported to have said was the seemingly meaningless words: 'There will be guests at the Hall.' Which she repeated more than once in an undertone.

Sir Matthew Fell was not unimpressed by the bearing of the woman. He had some talk upon the matter with the Vicar of his parish, with whom he travelled home after the assize business was over. His evidence at the trial had not been very willingly given; he was not specially infected with the witch-finding mania, but he declared, then and afterwards, that he could not give any other account of the matter than that he had given, and that he could not possibly have been mistaken as to what he saw. The whole transaction had been repugnant to him, for he was a man who liked to be on pleasant terms with those about him; but he saw a duty to be done in this business, and he had done it. That seems to have been the gist of his sentiments, and the Vicar applauded it, as any reasonable man must have done.

A few weeks after, when the moon of May was at the full, Vicar and Squire met again in the park, and walked to the Hall together. Lady Fell was with her mother, who was dangerously ill, and Sir Matthew was alone at home; so the Vicar, Mr Crome, was easily persuaded to take a late supper at the Hall.

Sir Matthew was not very good company this evening. The talk ran chiefly on family and parish matters, and, as luck would have it, Sir Matthew made a memorandum in writing of certain wishes or intentions of his regarding his estates, which afterwards proved exceedingly useful.

When Mr Crome thought of starting for home, about half-past nine o'clock, Sir Matthew and he took a preliminary turn on the gravelled walk at the back of the house. The only incident that struck Mr Crome was this: they were in sight of the ash-tree which I described as growing near the windows of the building, when Sir Matthew stopped and said:

'What is that that runs up and down the stem of the ash? It is never a squirrel? They will all be in their nests by now.'

The Vicar looked and saw the moving creature, but he could make nothing of its colour in the moonlight. The sharp outline, however, seen for an instant, was imprinted on his brain, and he could have sworn, he said, though it sounded foolish, that, squirrel or not, it had more than four legs.

Still, not much was to be made of the momentary vision, and the two men parted. They may have met since then, but it was not for a score of years.

Next day Sir Matthew Fell was not downstairs at six in the morning, as was his custom, nor at seven, nor yet at eight. Hereupon the servants went and knocked at his chamber door. I need not prolong the description of their anxious listenings and renewed batterings on the panels. The door was opened at last from the outside, and they found their master dead and black. So much you have guessed. That there were any marks of violence did not at the moment appear; but the window was open.

One of the men went to fetch the parson, and then by his directions rode on to give notice to the coroner. Mr Crome himself went as quick as he might to the Hall, and was shown to the room where the dead man lay. He has left some notes among his papers which show how genuine a respect and sorrow was felt for Sir Matthew, and there is also this passage, which I transcribe for the sake of the light it throws upon the course of events, and also upon the common beliefs of the time:

'There was not any the least Trace of an Entrance having been forc'd to the Chamber: but the Casement stood open, as my poor Friend would always have it in this Season. He had his Evening Drink of small Ale in a silver vessel of about a pint measure, and tonight had not drunk it out. This Drink was examined by the Physician from Bury, a Mr Hodgkins, who could not, however, as he afterwards declar'd upon his Oath, before the Coroner's quest, discover that any matter of a venomous kind was present in it. For, as was natural, in the great Swelling and Blackness of the Corpse, there was talk made among the Neighbours of Poyson. The Body was very much Disorder'd as it laid in the Bed, being twisted after so extream a sort as gave too probable Conjecture that my worthy Friend and Patron had expir'd in great Pain and Agony. And what is as yet unexplain'd, and to myself the Argument of some Horrid and Artfull Designe in the Perpetrators of this Barbarous Murther, was this, that the Women which were entrusted with the laying-out of the Corpse and washing it, being both sad Persons and very well Respected in their Mournfull Profession, came to me in a great Pain and Distress both of Mind and Body, saying, what was indeed confirmed upon the first View, that they had no sooner touch'd the Breast of the Corpse with their naked Hands than they were sensible of a more than ordinary violent Smart and Acheing in their Palms, which, with their whole Forearms, in no long time swell'd so immoderately, the Pain still continuing, that, as afterwards proved, during many weeks they were forc'd to lay by the exercise of their Calling; and yet no mark seen on the Skin.

'Upon hearing this, I sent for the Physician, who was still in the House, and we made as carefull a Proof as we were able by the Help of a small Magnifying Lens of Crystal of the condition of the Skinn on this Part of the Body: but could not detect with the Instrument we had any Matter of Importance beyond a couple of small Punctures or Pricks, which we then concluded were the Spotts by which the Poyson might be introduced, remembering that Ring of Pope Borgia, with other known Specimens of the Horrid Art of the Italian Poysoners of the last age.

'So much is to be said of the Symptoms seen on the Corpse. As to what I am to add, it is merely my own Experiment, and to be left to Posterity to judge whether there be anything of Value therein. There was on the Table by the Beddside a Bible of the small size, in which my Friend - punctuall as in Matters of less Moment, so in this more weighty one - used nightly, and upon his First Rising, to read a sett Portion. And I taking it up - not without a Tear duly paid to him which from the Study of this poorer Adumbration was now pass'd to the contemplation of its great Originall - it came into my Thoughts, as at such moments of Helplessness we are prone to catch at any the least Glimmer that makes promise of Light, to make trial of that old and by many accounted Superstitious Practice of drawing the Sortes: of which a Principall Instance, in the case of his late Sacred Majesty the Blessed Martyr King Charles and my Lord Falkland, was now much talked of. I must needs admit that by my Trial not much Assistance was afforded me: yet, as the Cause and Origin of these Dreadful Events may hereafter be search'd out, I set down the Results, in the case it may be found that they pointed the true Quarter of the Mischief to a quicker Intelligence than my own. ' I made, then, three trials, opening the Book and placing my Finger upon certain Words: which gave in the first these words, from Luke xiii 7, Cut it down; in the second, Isaiah xiii 20, It shall never be inhabited; and upon the third Experiment, Job xxxix 30, Her young ones also suck up blood.'

This is all that need be quoted from Mr Crome's papers. Sir Matthew Fell was duly coffined and laid into the earth, and his funeral sermon, preached by Mr Crome on the following Sunday, has been printed under the title of 'The Unsearchable Way; or, England's Danger and the Malicious Dealings of Anti-christ', it being the Vicar's view, as well as that most commonly held in the neighbourhood, that the Squire was the victim of a recrudescence of the Popish Plot.

His son, Sir Matthew the second, succeeded to the title and estates. And so ends the first act of the Castringham tragedy. It is to be mentioned, though the fact is not surprising, that the new Baronet did not occupy the room in which his father had died. Nor, indeed, was it slept in by anyone but an occasional visitor during the whole of his occupation. He died in 1735, and I do not find that anything particular marked his reign, save a curiously constant mortality among his cattle and livestock in general, which showed a tendency to increase slightly as time went on.

Those who are interested in the details will find a statistical account in a letter to the Gentleman's Magazine of 1772, which draws the facts from the Baronet's own papers. He put an end to it at last by a very simple expedient, that of shutting up all his beasts in sheds at night, and keeping no sheep in his park. For he had noticed that nothing was ever attacked that spent the night indoors. After that the disorder confined itself to wild birds, and beasts of chase. But as we have no good account of the symptoms, and as all-night watching was quite unproductive of any clue, I do not dwell on what the Suffolk farmers called the 'Castringham sickness'.

The second Sir Matthew died in 1735, as I said, and was duly succeeded by his son, Sir Richard. It was in his time that the great family pew was built out on the north side of the parish church. So large were the Squire's ideas that several of the graves on that unhallowed side of the building had to be disturbed to satisfy his requirements. Among them was that of Mrs Mothersole, the position of which was accurately known, thanks to a note on a plan of the church and yard, both made by Mr Crome.

A certain amount of interest was excited in the village when it was known that the famous witch, who was still remembered by a few, was to be exhumed. And the feeling of surprise, and indeed disquiet, was very strong when it was found that, though her coffin was fairly sound and unbroken, there was no trace whatever inside it of body, bones, or dust. Indeed, it is a curious phenomenon, for at the time of her burying no such things were dreamt of as resurrection-men, and it is difficult to conceive any rational motive for stealing a body otherwise than for the uses of the dissecting-room.

The incident revived for a time all the stories of witch-trials and of the exploits of the witches, dormant for forty years, and Sir Richard's orders that the coffin should be burnt were thought by a good many to be rather foolhardy, though they were duly carried out.

Sir Richard was a pestilent innovator, it is certain. Before his time the Hall had been a fine block of the mellowest red brick; but Sir Richard had travelled in Italy and become infected with the Italian taste, and, having more money than his predecessors, he determined to leave an Italian palace where he had found an English house. So stucco and ashlar masked the brick; some indifferent Roman marbles were planted about in the entrance-hall and gardens; a reproduction of the Sibyl's temple at Tivoli was erected on the opposite bank of the mere; and Castringham took on an entirely new, and, I must say, a less engaging, aspect. But it was much admired, and served as a model to a good many of the neighbouring gentry in after years.

One morning (it was in 1754) Sir Richard woke after a night of discomfort. It had been windy, and his chimney had smoked persistently, and yet it was so cold that he must keep up a fire. Also something had so rattled about the window that no man could get a moment's peace. Further, there was the prospect of several guests of position arriving in the course of the day, who would expect sport of some kind, and the inroads of the distemper (which continued among his game) had been lately so serious that he was afraid for his reputation as a game-preserver. But what really touched him most nearly was the other matter of his sleepless night. He could certainly not sleep in that room again.

That was the chief subject of his meditations at breakfast, and after it he began a systematic examination of the rooms to see which would suit his notions best. It was long before he found one. This had a window with an eastern aspect and that with a northern; this door the servants would be always passing, and he did not like the bedstead in that. No, he must have a room with a western look-out, so that the sun could not wake him early, and it must be out of the way of the business of the house. The housekeeper was at the end of her resources. 'Well, Sir Richard,' she said, 'you know that there is but one room like that in the house.' 'Which may that be?' said Sir Richard. 'And that is Sir Matthew's – the West Chamber.' 'Well, put me in there, for there I'll lie tonight,' said her master. 'Which way is it? Here, to be sure'; and he hurried off.

'Oh, Sir Richard, but no one has slept there these forty years. The air has hardly been changed since Sir Matthew died there.' Thus she spoke, and rustled after him. 'Come, open the door, Mrs Chiddock. I'll see the chamber, at least.'

So it was opened, and, indeed, the smell was very close and earthy. Sir Richard crossed to the window, and, impatiently, as was his wont, threw the shutters back, and flung open the casement. For this end of the house was one which the alterations had barely touched, grown up as it was with the great ash-tree, and being otherwise concealed from view.

'Air it, Mrs Chiddock, all today, and move my bed-furniture in in the afternoon. Put the Bishop of Kilmore in my old room.'

'Pray, Sir Richard,' said a new voice, breaking in on this speech, 'might I have the favour of a moment's interview?'

Sir Richard turned round and saw a man in black in the doorway, who bowed. 'I must ask your indulgence for this intrusion, Sir Richard. You will, perhaps, hardly remember me. My name is William Crome, and my grandfather was Vicar here in your grandfather's time.'

'Well, sir,' said Sir Richard, 'the name of Crome is always a passport to Castringham. I am glad to renew a friendship of two generations' standing. In what can I serve you? for your hour of calling – and, if I do not mistake you, your bearing – shows you to be in some haste.'

'That is no more than the truth, sir. I am riding from Norwich to Bury St Edmunds with what haste I can make, and I have called in on my way to leave with you some papers which we have but just come upon in looking over what my grandfather left at his death. It is thought you may find some matters of family interest in them.'

'You are mighty obliging, Mr Crome, and, if you will be so good as to follow me to the parlour, and drink a glass of wine, we will take a first look at these same papers together. And you, Mrs Chiddock, as I said, be about airing this chamber... Yes, it is here my grandfather died... Yes, the tree, perhaps, does make the place a little dampish... No; I do not wish to listen to any more. Make no difficulties, I beg. You have your orders – go. Will you follow me, sir?'

They went to the study. The packet which young Mr Crome had brought – he was then just become a Fellow of Clare Hall in Cambridge, I may say, and subsequently brought out a respectable edition of Polyaenus – contained among other things the notes which the old Vicar had made upon the occasion of Sir Matthew Fell's death. And for the first time Sir Richard was confronted with the enigmatical Sortes Biblicae which you have heard. They amused him a good deal.

'Well,' he said, 'my grandfather's Bible gave one prudent piece of advice – Cut it down. If that stands for the ash-tree, he may rest assured I shall not neglect it. Such a nest of catarrhs and agues was never seen.'

The parlour contained the family books, which, pending the arrival of a collection which Sir Richard had made in Italy, and the building of a proper room to receive them, were not many in number.

Sir Richard looked up from the paper to the bookcase.

'I wonder,' says he, 'whether the old prophet is there yet? I fancy I see him.'

Crossing the room, he took out a dumpy Bible, which, sure enough, bore on the flyleaf the inscription: 'To Matthew Fell, from his Loving Godmother, Anne Aldous, 2 September, 1659.'

'It would be no bad plan to test him again, Mr Crome. I will wager we get a couple of names in the Chronicles. H'm! what have we here? "Thou shalt seek me in the morning, and I shall not be." Well, well! Your grandfather would have made a fine omen of that, hey? No more prophets for me! They are all in a tale. And now, Mr Crome, I am infinitely obliged to you for your packet. You will, I fear, be impatient to get on. Pray allow me – another glass.' So with offers of hospitality, which were genuinely meant (for Sir Richard thought well of the young man's address and manner), they parted.

In the afternoon came the guests – the Bishop of Kilmore, Lady Mary Hervey, Sir William Kentfield, etc. Dinner at five, wine, cards, supper, and dispersal to bed.

Next morning Sir Richard is disinclined to take his gun with the rest. He talks with the Bishop of Kilmore. This prelate, unlike a good many of the Irish Bishops of his day, had visited his see, and, indeed, resided there for some considerable time. This morning, as the two were walking along the terrace and talking over the alterations and improvements in the house, the Bishop said, pointing to the window of the West Room:

'You could never get one of my Irish flock to occupy that room, Sir Richard.'

'Why is that, my lord? It is, in fact, my own.'

'Well, our Irish peasantry will always have it that it brings the worst of luck to sleep near an ash-tree, and you have a fine growth of ash not two yards from your chamber window. Perhaps,' the Bishop went on, with a smile, 'it has given you a touch of its quality already, for you do not seem, if I may say it, so much the fresher for your night's rest as your friends would like to see you.'

'That, or something else, it is true, cost me my sleep from twelve to four, my lord. But the tree is to come down tomorrow, so I shall not hear much more from it.'

'I applaud your determination. It can hardly be wholesome to have the air you breathe strained, as it were, through all that leafage.'

'Your lordship is right there, I think. But I had not my window open last night. It was rather the noise that went on – no doubt from the twigs sweeping the glass – that kept me open-eyed.'

'I think that can hardly be. Sir Richard. Here – you see it from this point. None of these nearest branches even can touch your casement unless there were a gale, and there was none of that last night. They miss the panes by a foot.'

'No, sir, true. What, then, will it be, I wonder, that scratched and rustled so – ay, and covered the dust on my sill with lines and marks?'

At last they agreed that the rats must have come up through the ivy. That was the Bishop's idea, and Sir Richard jumped at it.

So the day passed quietly, and night came, and the party dispersed to their rooms, and wished Sir Richard a better night.

And now we are in his bedroom, with the light out and the Squire in bed. The room is over the kitchen, and the night outside still and warm, so the window stands open.

There is very little light about the bedstead, but there is a strange movement there; it seems as if Sir Richard were moving his head rapidly to and fro with only the slightest possible sound. And now you would guess, so deceptive is the half-darkness, that he had several heads, round and brownish, which move back and forward, even as low as his chest. It is a horrible illusion. Is it nothing more? There! something drops off the bed with a soft plump, like a kitten, and is out of the window in a flash; another – four – and after that there is quiet again.

'Thou shalt seek me in the morning, and I shall not be.'

As with Sir Matthew, so with Sir Richard – dead and black in his bed! A pale and silent party of guests and servants gathered under the window when the news was known. Italian poisoners, Popish emissaries, infected air – all these and more guesses were hazarded, and the Bishop of Kilmore looked at the tree, in the fork of whose lower boughs a white tom-cat was crouching, looking down the hollow which years had gnawed in the trunk. It was watching something inside the tree with great interest.

Suddenly it got up and craned over the hole. Then a bit of the edge on which it stood gave way, and it went slithering in. Everyone looked up at the noise of the fall.

It is known to most of us that a cat can cry; but few of us have heard, I hope, such a yell as came out of the trunk of the great ash. Two or three screams there were – the witnesses are not sure which – and then a slight and muffled noise of some commotion or struggling was all that came. But Lady Mary Hervey fainted outright, and the housekeeper stopped her ears and fled till she fell on the terrace,

The Bishop of Kilmore and Sir William Kentfield stayed. Yet even they were daunted, though it was only at the cry of a cat; and Sir William swallowed once or twice before he could say:

'There is something more than we know of in that tree, my lord. I am for an instant search.' And this was agreed upon. A ladder was brought, and one of the gardeners went up, and, looking down the hollow, could detect nothing but a few dim indications of something moving. They got a lantern, and let it down by a rope.

'We must get at the bottom of this. My life upon it, my lord, but the secret of these terrible deaths is there.'

Up went the gardener again with the lantern, and let it down the hole cautiously. They saw the yellow light upon his face as he bent over, and saw his face struck with an incredulous terror and loathing before he cried out in a dreadful voice and fell back from the ladder – where, happily, he was caught by two of the men – letting the lantern fall inside the tree. He was in a dead faint, and it was some time before any word could be got from him. By then they had something else to look at. The lantern must have broken at the bottom, and the light in it caught upon dry leaves and rubbish that lay there, for in a few minutes a dense smoke began to come up, and then flame; and, to be short, the tree was in a blaze. The bystanders made a ring at some yards' distance, and Sir William and the Bishop sent men to get what weapons and tools they could; for, clearly, whatever might be using the tree as its lair would be forced out by the fire.

So it was. First, at the fork, they saw a round body covered with fire – the size of a man's head – appear very suddenly, then seem to collapse and fall back. This, five or six times; then a similar ball leapt into the air and fell on the grass, where after a moment it lay still. The Bishop went as near as he dared to it, and saw – what but the remains of an enormous spider, veinous and seared! And, as the fire burned lower down, more terrible bodies like this began to break out from the trunk, and it was seen that these were covered with greyish hair.

All that day the ash burned, and until it fell to pieces the men stood about it, and from time to time killed the brutes as they darted out. At last there was a long interval when none appeared, and they cautiously closed in and examined the roots of the tree. 'They found,' says the Bishop of Kilmore, 'below it a rounded hollow place in the earth, wherein were two or three bodies of these creatures that had plainly been smothered by the smoke; and, what is to me more curious, at the side of this den, against the wall, was crouching the anatomy or skeleton of a human being, with the skin dried upon the bones, having some remains of black hair, which was pronounced by those that examined it to be undoubtedly the body of a woman, and clearly dead for a period of fifty years.'

MARI LWYD

By Thomas Alexander

The horse spirit Mari Lwyd is often found in Wales at Christmas time, tradition says if it bests you in rhyme or song it must be invited in to eat...

Is it a pleasant visit, or something more sinister? Will we find out in this new short story from Italian author Thomas Alexander?

MARI LWYD

Mari Lwyd's skull was adorned by bells, and those bells all chimed in unison when they walked. Their mantle, a white cloth, protected them from the heavy snow pouring down the streets of Crumlin.

December this year was cold and unforgiving, an anomaly these days, and the horse spirit definitely felt it. They shivered as they walked down the private street towards the yellow house they just eyed.

Despite not having a nervous system. Or skin. Or anything that wasn't off-white, cracked bones. The cold was more of a state of mind, honestly.

They knocked on the wooden door, patiently waiting for an answer, one that took a few minutes to come, but for a good reason: a boy opened the green door, with his little hands grabbing the door handle like their life depended on it and looking up to the creature with awe, mouth slightly agape.

There now follows the usual routine: Mari Lwyd starts chanting, the little kid tries to respond, stumbling over a few words as he recites the songs his parents taught him in the case the horse came to visit, and this repeats until one can continue no more and has to concede.

In the middle of his second rebuttal, as he's trying to say a word a little too advanced for his age without tying his tongue in a knot, the little kid throws his hands up in the air, concedes, and invites Mari in.

"Sit down, I'm making you hot chocolate." He simply says as

Mari Lwyd enters the cozy home.

Oh, that worries them. A kid as young as him, near a stovetop? Having to fetch items from the higher shelves? Yeah... no. That's several incidents waiting to happen.

Wordlessly, they follow the kid in the kitchen and patiently watch as he retrieves the hot chocolate packet, only to step in the help the boy take the pot out of the pantry and turn the gas on. They carefully watch as the boy pours all the contents needed in the pot, stirring messily with a wooden spoon and splashing milk all over the counter.

"My parents went to visit my grandma, she lives down the street." The boy informs Mari Lwyd, and thanks his deity. They hope the parent will be back soon, and wonder what could have happened to the kid if they hadn't knocked and he was left unattended. Nothing good, that's for sure.

"So now we wait five minutes..." The boy says as he jumps off the chair Mari put in front of the stove. The boy runs for the pantry, where he stretches and manages to take two plastic mugs, one themed around the Muppets, with baby Kermit and Miss Piggy sitting on a bench and playing, and a Christmas one, with the reindeers, Santa, and all, from the third-highest shelf.

Mari Lwyd got the Muppet mug.

"It's bubbling. Does that mean it's ready?" the boys asks. Mari slowly nods and picks up the pot, pouring an equal amount of hot chocolate in the two mugs. The little boy is beaming as he watches. "Do you want whipped cream on it?" He beelines to the fridge, and after a bit of struggling, opens the fridge door and pulls out a half-empty can of spray whipped cream.

Mari Lwyd nods again.

Finally, they sit at the living room table and drink.

Mari Lwyd, being the ancient spirit of a horse skeleton, shouldn't really be able to drink the hot chocolate, as they have no organs or digestive system. But somehow they do. Maybe the love and excitement the little kid put into the drink magically changed their anatomy, or maybe it's best not to ask questions about the specificities of a mythical creature.

Finally, after a few minutes of sitting and drinking at the table, during which the kid turned on the TV and started showing Mari his favourite cartoons, they heard the sound of chattering and keys turning at the main entrance of the house.

"Hey, Kevin, how did-" The kid's father takes one second to register Mari Lwyd's presence, but when he does he looks more annoyed than anything else. "Lois." He says to his wife "They're back."

KRAMPUS' EVE

By Barney Butler

American author Barney Butler is a fan of European folklore and schlock horror. He lists Krampus as one of her favourite Christmas movies and has written a homage to the movie in this new story appearing for the fist time in this anthology.

KRAMPUS' EVE

I

The glow of holiday cheer radiates through the room as Jack Sherbourne arranges garlands of twinkling lights, their warm glow casting a soft ambiance whilst his wife Emily adorns the pine tree with a myriad of ornaments, each one holding memories of Christmases past.

Seated at the table, their daughter Skye sits with a determined gleam in her eye as her pen dances across the paper, etching her desires with unwavering fervour.

"Hey there, kiddo," Jack called out with a grin, eyeing Skye's intense scribbling. "What's got you so engrossed over there?"

Skye glanced up, her face lighting up. "It's my letter to Santa! I've got to make sure he knows exactly what I want."

"And what are your heart's desires this year, my dear?" Emily asked, smiling.

"A bicycle! The one with the sparkly pink handlebars and a bell," Skye exclaimed, her enthusiasm palpable. "Oh, and a basket for Daisy, too!"

Nana Mary, seated nearby, chuckled softly. "Quite the wish list, dear. But Santa does love a child who dreams big."

Gramps Hamish, nodding in agreement, added, "Absolutely. And he's always listening to the kind-hearted ones, too."

Jack, his grin widening, interjected, "Santa might need an extra sleigh this year if that list gets much longer?"

"But he's magic, Dad! He can make anything happen." Skye stated with the absolute belief an eight year old can muster.

Emily, in a gentle tone, reminded Skye, "Remember dear, Christmas isn't just about what we receive. It's also about sharing joy and kindness."

Skye nodded vigorously. "I'll make sure to tell Santa that too!"

The doorbell's chime broke the festive rhythm, surprising the household.

Emily hurried to the door. "Rebecca?" she uttered, the name tinged with uncertainty as she saw her younger sister standing in front of her. “I wasn’t expecting you?”

"Surprise, Em!" Rebecca's voice carried a hint of cheeriness as she stepped inside, her three children in tow. "Sorry to arrive unannounced, a little trouble on-going between hubby and I. Hope it's not a bad time!"

Jack approached with a welcoming smile. "Never a bad time for family, Rebecca. Come on in!"

Tommy and Beth darted past their aunt, eager to explore the unfamiliar surroundings, while baby Abby nestled contentedly in Rebecca's arms.

"And who might this mischievous fellow be?" Jack chuckled, gesturing towards a feline figure sauntering through the doorway.

Rebecca laughed. "Oh, that's Whiskers. Our troublemaker," she explained as the curious cat made itself at home.

In the midst of the commotion, a figure emerged from the shadows, clad in eclectic attire and exuding an air of enigmatic allure. "Martha," Emily exclaimed with a mixture of surprise and warmth, embracing her peculiar yet beloved aunt.

"Emily, dear! It's been too long," Martha greeted, her voice carrying an otherworldly timbre that piqued curiosity.

As the Sherbourne household welcomed the unexpected guests, a whirlwind of greetings and laughter filled the room, brushing aside the tension caused by the unexpected arrival. Skye, eager to share her festive spirit with her cousins, bounded towards them with her letter in hand. "Look, I wrote to Santa!" Her eyes sparkled with excitement.

But her cousins, Tommy and Beth, exchanged a knowing glance, their expressions veiled in mocking amusement. "Santa?" Tommy scoffed. "You still believe in that stuff?"

Skye's enthusiasm faltered, her heart sinking at their ridicule. "It's not stuff, it's magic!" Her voice trembled with frustration.

Rebecca attempted to intervene gently, "Come on, kids, let's not ruin Skye's excitement."

But Beth, fuelled by her brothers air of mockery, joined in, "Yeah, magic that doesn't exist! You're such a baby."

The sting of their words pierced Skye's joy, a surge of pent-up emotions flooding her. "I hate this! I hate all of you and I hate stupid Christmas!" Her outburst echoed through the room, leaving an uncomfortable silence in its wake.

Emily rushed to Skye's side, trying to console her amidst the growing tension. "Skye, sweetie, it's okay. We all just need a moment."

The air grew heavy with Skye's disillusionment, her mood changing suddenly to a fierce disdain for the family and the festive season. Amidst the strained silence, Skye's outburst lingered, the tension thickening like an unspoken storm waiting to break.

Jack, his heart aching for his daughter, approached Skye with a gentle touch. "Hey, kiddo, I know it's tough. But family's important, even when things get tough."

Skye, her eyes brimming with tears of frustration, snatched her crumpled letter from Jack's hand, her emotions a whirlwind. "It's not fair!" Her voice quivered with indignation.

Emily tried to reason with Skye. "Sweetheart, sometimes we have to find a way to understand each other, even when it's hard."

But Skye, consumed by her feelings, felt a surge of anger and helplessness. In a sudden fit of emotion, she tore the letter to shreds, stomping to the front door to hurl the torn pieces into the sky, as if to release her disillusionment and hurt into the vast expanse above.

The shattered remnants of Skye's letter floated away, scattering like snowflakes in the night.

11

As darkness descended on Christmas Eve an unexpected blizzard, relentless and unforgiving, swept through the streets, blanketing everything in a shroud of icy white.

Skye, her heart heavy with the day's turmoil, snuck out into the biting cold night, determined to prove her cousins wrong, to catch a glimpse of Santa Claus. But not far past the end of her yard she became disoriented, a chilling sensation washed over her. Skye hurried through the snowy veil, her footsteps muffled by the thick snow, but she felt something —a presence— looming in the shadows, watching, waiting.

Her breaths quickened as she glimpsed the looming, horned figure amidst the storm, its silhouette hauntingly familiar. Panic seized her, and she spotted shelter—a rundown cabin that seemed to appear out of nowhere in the blinding snow.

Once inside, Skye's racing heart sought solace, but a strange unease settled in the air. A shiver ran down her spine as eerie toys began to materialize around her—a jack-in-the-box, a doll that seemed to move of its own accord, their innocent facades warped into something unsettling in the dim light.

The cabin, once a refuge, now felt like an otherworldly stage where the toys' presence grew more ominous with each passing moment, their eyes seeming to follow her every move, a surreal and haunting spectacle in the heart of the blizzard's icy grip.

Alone in the chilling embrace of the rundown cabin, Skye found herself thrust into a surreal nightmare, the eerie toys a haunting reminder that she was not alone, lost in the wintry darkness that engulfed the town.

III

"Skye! Skye!" Emily shouts into the biting wind, her concern rapidly growing into fear.

"Emily, wait!" her sister calls, "Don't go too far, let's not lose each other in this snow."

"She must be out here somewhere Rebecca. We need to find her."

"Look, that cabin." Rebecca points, "Could she have gone in there?"

"This can't be right" Emily replies, "I don't remember a cabin so close to the house. Come on, let's check."

The cabin loomed before them, its shattered windows and strange tracks in the snow making Rebecca shiver.

"Em, something feels wrong." Rebecca said, her voice trembling.

"Skye, are you in there?" Emily called out.

Rebecca peered through the frosted windowpanes, her breath fogging the glass. "Em, look!"

Emily hurried over, her heart pounding with apprehension. Through the window, they spotted Skye, huddled in a corner, her eyes wide with fear.

"Skye!" Rebecca called out, her voice muffled by the howling wind.

Emily rattled the door, but it was firmly shut. "She's trapped in there. We have to get her out!"

With a determined shove, Rebecca pushed against the door, the old wood groaning under the strain. Finally, it gave way, and they rushed inside.

"Skye, sweetheart, it's us!" Emily called out, her voice a reassuring beacon.

Skye's tear-streaked face lit up with relief. "Mom! Aunt Rebecca!"

A distant growl cut through the reunion, freezing them in place.

“What in the world was that?” Rebecca exclaimed.

“Mom” Skye said, “I'm scared”

Suddenly, nearby, an otherworldly growl echoed, piercing through the blizzard. Rebecca's instincts kicked in, propelling her to shield Emily just in time, narrowly evading the unseen threat.

Grabbing Skye's arm she shouted “We need to move. Now!”

With hearts pounding they raced back through the storm, seeking refuge within the confines of their home, their thoughts clouded with worry and an inexplicable sense of impending doom.

“What was out there?” Rebecca said, her voice shaking.

“I don't know,” Emily replied, “but it's not safe.”

“Krampus” Gramps Hamish's voice cut through with a solemn weight.

"Once, in my childhood village," Gramps Hamish continued "Christmas held a magic that brightened every heart. But as the world outside beckoned, our village began to lose its festive glow."

“We don’t have time for your reminiscing now Gramps” Emily cut in.

“Wait child, hear me out” Gramps Hamish snapped back, before continuing "Arthur, my closest friend, was among those leaving for the cities, our village was enveloped in a cloud of desolation, and the spirit of Christmas began to fade."

Emily, her brow furrowed in concern, listened intently to her father's tale.

"I remember our falling out," Gramps Hamish's voice held a hint of remorse. "Arthur and his family were set to depart in the New Year. In a moment of childish frustration, I uttered words that summoned Krampus, wishing for Arthur to be taken now rather than later."

The room grew eerily silent as the gravity of his words settled.

"Krampus and his dark cohorts," Gramps Hamish continued, his tone heavy with remorse, "descended upon Arthur's home. They snatched him and his family away to a realm beyond, leaving behind only bell-shaped baubles as a haunting reminder of their departure."

"I don't think we have to worry about Krampus, Gramps," Tommy chuckled, he was too grown up to believe in Santa, his youthful bravado wasn't going to believe in ghost stories.

Beth, eyes wide with concern, glanced around the room, "It's just a story, right?" she was a couple of years younger, still smarting from her older brother Tommy snatching the gift of belief away from her

But as she spoke the gifts they had exchanged earlier began to stir with an eerie animation, the action figure dangling from Tommy's hand seconds previously now biting into his finger causing him to yelp out in pain.

Rebecca's voice rose in alarm. "Tommy!"

Whiskers, the family's beloved pet cat, transformed from a docile companion into a creature of malevolent intent, its eyes gleaming with an otherworldly ferocity. With a startling swiftness, Whiskers lunged at Beth, hissing and clawing with an unsettling aggression.

Rebecca's voice cracked now with fear. "Whiskers, what's gotten into you?!"

Amidst the chaotic struggle against the animated toys, Martha's voice pierced through the mayhem, her tone wrought with both fear and determination. "Beth, come to me!"

Beth, her wide eyes reflecting both confusion and dread, made a desperate dash towards her aunt, attempting to evade the menacing grasp of the eerie elves materializing from the shadowy corners of the room. With a swift, chilling efficiency, the sinister beings closed in, their wiry fingers extending like tendrils of darkness, clutching at the little girl's sleeves.

Martha lunged forward, arms outstretched, but the elusive creatures moved with an otherworldly agility. "No, Beth! Hold on!"

"Martha, Beth!" Rebecca's voice rang out, her eyes wide with disbelief and terror.

Emily's frantic calls echoed in the room. "Hold on, we're coming!"

But despite their desperate attempts, the eerie elves whisked Martha and Beth away, vanishing into the obscure depths of the room, leaving a haunting emptiness in their wake.

The family stood frozen, their efforts futile against the malevolent forces that had snatched their loved ones away, leaving behind silence, tainted with grief.

IV

"We need to get out of here," Jack's voice resonated with urgency, his eyes scanning for a means of escape.

Tommy clung tightly to his mother, teenage bravado forgotten and fear now etched on his face. "Where do we go?"

Emily, her gaze determined, stepped forward. "Just get out, I'll stay behind to distract him."

As the family hastily made their way towards the front door, Emily stayed behind, a beacon of bravery in the face of looming darkness. With steady determination, she prepared herself to confront the ominous figure that emerged from the chimney, wielding a sinister bag of cursed toys.

The room fell into a tense silence as Emily squared her shoulders, unknown courage propelling her forward to face the emerging threat. She steeled herself for the daunting task of distracting Krampus, knowing that her sacrifice might buy her family the precious moments they needed to escape the chilling clutches of the malevolent entity.

As the Sherbourne family raced through the biting cold, their breaths visible in the frosty air, the elements seemed to conspire against them. Krampus' sinister snow monsters and eerie elves encircled them, trapping the family in a suffocating vortex of snow and darkness.

"We're surrounded!" Rebecca's voice trembled.

Jack, his jaw set with a steely resolve, pushed through the swirling snow, trying to shield his family from the encroaching creatures. "Keep moving! We have to find a way out!"But their escape was thwarted at every turn, the malevolent forces closing in, their intentions unmistakably sinister.

Meanwhile, near a blazing pit, Krampus loomed menacingly, his towering figure casting an ominous shadow over Tommy. The flickering flames illuminated the daunting confrontation as Tommy, driven by sheer desperation, faced off against the spectral entity.

Skye, overwhelmed with guilt for her impulsive actions that had led to this dire situation, stepped forward, her voice quivering yet determined. "It's because of me. Take me instead."

Jack's eyes widened in disbelief as Skye bravely confronted Krampus, her sacrifice a testament to her love for her family.

The air crackled with tension as Skye, her voice barely above a whisper, pleaded with Krampus. "I'm sorry," her eyes were brimming with tears. "I never meant for this to happen. Please, let them go. Take me instead."

Jack, torn between anguish and admiration for his daughter's courage, stood frozen, his heart aching with the weight of the moment as Skye bravely offered herself in exchange for her family's safety.

Krampus, momentarily swayed by Skye's genuine remorse, appeared to relent. His expression softened, hinting at a flicker of empathy. But then, with deliberation, just as he appeared to accept her apology he hurled her into the fiery abyss below with a twisted grin.

As Skye hurtled into the void, terror and regret consumed her. Abruptly, she bolted upright in her bed, gasping for breath on Christmas morning. Racing downstairs, relief washed over her at the sight of her family, seemingly unscathed after the harrowing night and carrying on their Christmas morning as if nothing had happened.

But among the glittering decorations on the mantelpiece stood an oddity—a Christmas card that hadn't been there before. Rebecca, with a curious tilt of her head, was the first to notice.

"Hey, what's this?" she questioned, picking up the peculiar card. “I didn’t notice this here yesterday”

Jack, intrigued, joined her. "That's new. Looks like..."

"Like our house," Emily finished his sentence, a note of disbelief in her voice.

The family gathered around, peering closely at the image. It showed a reflection of their home stood frozen in time.

Emily leaned in, her breath catching. "Look it's us... through the window there... you can see us clustered around the card."

Skye, her eyes wide with dread, scanned the miniature scene.

“Krampus” Gramps Hamish stated, a chill settling within the room.

“You remember Gramps?” Skye's voice trembled. "Does that mean we're being watched?"

Rebecca's eyes widened as she suddenly remembered the events of the previous night. "We can't stay here! How do we get out?"

Jack's jaw clenched, as memories came flooding back to him too. "We'll figure it out. We can't be stuck here."

Printed in Great Britain
by Amazon

36220720R00118